REAPER TWO-SIX

- YEAR 6 -

ACT OF
REDEMPTION

Robert A. Grand

Copyright © 2012-2013 by Robert A. Grand
Reaper Two-Six® is a registered trademark by Robert A. Grand

Cover illustration by Jeremy Blackston and Robert Grand
Editors: Carol Bates, Priscilla Johnson and J. Conrad Guest

ISBN-13: 978-0983824725

Library of Congress Control Number: 2012921167

Printed in the United States of America
First edition: November 2012
Second edition: January 2013
Second edition, second printing: September 2013

Published by:
Reaper Two-Six Productions
South Lyon, Michigan 48178

Email: productions@reapertwosix.com
www.reapertwosixproductions.com

PREFACE

The threat of worldwide terrorism demands that governments around the globe spend more and more of their precious capital on the security of their citizens. The resulting economic impact cripples nations; they struggle to manage commerce, international trade, business growth, job creation, and tourism. The world economy is on the brink of collapse.

In response to overwhelming international pressure, NATO+ creates the Global Defense Organization (GDO). The hand-picked GDO leaders — call signs Wolverine, PVL, and Loz — form Reaper Two-Six®: an elite forty-eight member multinational covert squadron.

The Reapers, as they're known, are all top military pilots from countries around the globe. Many having additional specialties — ground operations, snipers, communications, reconnaissance, and intelligence gathering.

The GDO's singular purpose: eliminate worldwide terrorism.

GDO Organizational Chart

(At the end of year 5)

Global Headquarters: Argyle, Michigan USA
Commanded by Fleet Admiral Wolverine
Eastern Command: Stavoren, Netherlands
Commanded by Admiral PVL
Western Command: Carnarvon, Western Australia
Commanded by Vice Admiral Loz

Reaper Two-Six Members (Country from)

Captains

DaXx (Croatia)   **Doc** (U.S.)   **Professor** (U.S.)
Ranger (Singapore) **Red Diamond** (Scotland)   **Viral** (Canada)

Commanders

Blast (Panama)   **Cloud** (England)   **Fox** (Netherlands)
Gunner (Netherlands) **LiangShan** (Taiwan)   **Magic** (Greece)
Pop (England)

LT Commanders

Buckshot (U.S.)   **Endo** (Canada)   **Ghost** (England)
Lucid (U.S.)   **Maniac** (U.S.)   **Scorch** (U.S.)
Shadow (U.S.)   **Sijei** (U.S.)   **Talon** (England)
Viper (England)

Lieutenants

25 total

To honor the military heritage of the GDO leaders, Reaper Two-Six adopted a naval ranking system.

ACKNOWLEDGEMENTS

I'm forever grateful to Carol Bates and Priscilla Johnson. Their patience, devotion, and willingness to support me allowed this book to be published. I love you both.

To my friends Jeremy Blackston, Jurian Janssen, and Benjamin Lawrence: your dedication, inspiration, and energy fostered me to keep writing. Your comments and reviews, throughout the creation of this book, were greatly appreciated.

I am thankful to my graphic artist Jeremy Blackston. His wonderful work shines on the cover of this book.

To my friends Peter Van Leeuwen and Lawrence Adcock: your devotion and passion for Reaper Two-Six encouraged me to try new things. Thank you for including me in your lives and for your tremendous support.

In any country, on any ocean, the Reapers are ready to serve.

Chapter 1
Sleight of Hand

Somewhere over southwestern Nevada, United States

"One minute." Doc yells into the communication system of the 727 cargo jet. The echo of her voice throughout the fuselage brings the reality of the whole situation into focus, while beads of sweat pool at the small of her back. The anticipation is brutal.

Nearly a year ago, the Reapers made a significant impact on world affairs, but as a secret covert squadron of the Global Defense Organization (GDO), the Reapers technically don't exist. Now, if all goes according to plan, they are about to shock the world again with a mission so far under cover that the top leaders of the original GDO know nothing about it. This caused quite a heated debate between Doc and Professor prior to take off, but the time to back out was way past and the time to deploy is at hand.

We're really going to do this aren't we? she thinks to herself as she makes final checks on the various dials and gauges on the cockpit panel in front of her.

Fear ran right down to her toes, but it was rapidly replaced by the excitement of knowing she would soon pilot a top secret hypersonic stealth aircraft. The fear wasn't because she didn't think she could handle the big bird; her dream had always been to fly the biggest and the baddest jets she could find. Feeling the stealth aircraft controls in her hands would be heaven. The fear was due to the fact that she would be *stealing* a top secret hypersonic jet from the United States of America. That was an act of treason, and she didn't particularly care to live out the rest of her days in Leavenworth.

After setting the 727's autopilot, Doc places her helmet loosely on her head, slips on her gloves and carefully shuffles her five-foot, eight-inch frame through the tight cockpit. With nylon fabric sewn between her legs and under her arms, along with insulated gloves and boots, Doc's high performance wingsuit completely envelops her soft mahogany skin.

She eases her way through the cockpit door, taking care not to snag her suit on any sharp edges. Slowly, like a duck out of water, she begins waddling through the partially lit cargo bay area, trying to not step on her delicate wingsuit.

A distant Halloween memory comes unbidden to her mind. When her parents moved to the United States from India, Doc was five years old, and her brother was only three. For her first Halloween, her mother made a hand-sewn duck costume, which made walking nearly impossible.

Doc shakes her head with a small smile playing about on her lips. *I wonder why I'm thinking about that,* she muses.

As she continues her awkward shuffle toward the rear of the aircraft, she grins in the dim light, imagining how she must look. *Certainly more like a duck than a skydiver in high tech gear,* she thinks.

The wingsuit's baggy fabric swishes along the floor, threatening to trip her at any moment.

The plan, after her jump, is for the aircraft to continue on its westerly heading, eventually taking it over central California. Then, when the fuel tanks run dry, the 727 will crash into the Pacific Ocean, eighty to a hundred miles off-shore.

Hours earlier, before she left eastern Texas, Doc filed a valid flight plan with the FAA. Officially, the 727 was a military cargo flight with a pilot, co-pilot and flight engineer. In reality, Doc and Professor are alone on this mission, and the aircraft is completely empty aside from the equipment they will carry with them when they jump.

The crash of a military cargo jet will be news-worthy, but the Reapers don't anticipate more than a few small search and rescue missions for survivors. The cover of a military cargo flight also gives Doc the clearance to fly close to the

Air Force Flight Test Center, where the target aircraft sits in its hanger.

For this mission, Doc programmed the autopilot to skim the edge of the no-fly zone.

Catching a shadowy glimpse of Doc approaching him, Professor reaches up and pulls the handle to open the rear door of the cargo 727. The whoosh of air from within the cabin nearly sucks him out. Tightening his grip on the handholds, he steadies himself, preparing for the opening of the rear stairway.

"Could have warned me," Doc yells, growling as she grasps the side rail.

As the highest ranking female Reaper, Doc takes a lot of abuse from her fellow mates. The typical bantering and crude jokes are to be expected. After all, piloting for an elite black ops organization like Reaper Two-Six is very competitive.

Lately, Professor has been pushing the limits of those competitive boundaries, which Doc feels is unnecessary given the high danger level of this mission.

The mission, she sighs. It used to be a sense of pride for her whenever she embarked on a mission for the Reapers. After all, she gave the organization her life. She put everything on hold to be a member: friends, family and love.

Reaper Two-Six
Year 6

That all came crashing down ten months ago on the day PVL fired her.

Doc feels the familiar sting behind her eyes at the memory. Those words from her commander haunt her every waking moment, along with a sense of failure. The Reapers were her life and now, without them...

She shakes her head in disbelief at what she's about to do.

"Fifteen seconds." Professor shouts.

The echo of his voice rings through the barren aircraft's fuselage shaking Doc to her senses. She narrows her eyes in a razor stare and smacks the tops of Professor's shoulders with her fists ... she's focused and ready.

As if saying goodbye, Professor turns his head to face Doc, nods, then yanks the release handle. The 727's rear stairway snaps open and begins to tremble violently in the four hundred knot wind.

The previously smooth flight changes abruptly as the aircraft aggressively shudders and shakes, its carefully pressurized hull breached by the open hatch. Triggered by the tail section bouncing around from the stairway's forceful gyrations and the sudden rush of air spewing from the rear of the plane, Doc and Professor are knocked off their feet.

Quickly tightening their hold on the side rails, the two Reapers desperately try to maintain their balance. With the plane jolting around, Doc loses her grip and is tossed across the floor, crashing into the lavatory door. Professor's impeccable reflexes snag her, keeping Doc from bouncing down the interior walls and sustaining serious injury. Bracing himself against the open doorway, he reaches out and sets her upright. Doc swiftly turns and looks Professor in the eyes, nodding to tell him she's all right.

Fearful their wingsuits might get damaged if they wait any longer, they prepare to jump. Professor clicks his GPS system on and immediately the Google glasses come to life within his helmet. Since he is still inside the aircraft's metal fuselage, the GPS signal is blocked. But once in freefall, the glasses will give him a clear view of the terrain below. He traverses down the wobbly stairway and leaps out into open air.

At first, the sensation of falling grips him with fear nearly paralyzing his body and mind. His years of training, both as an expert pilot and high altitude skydiver, take over and calm his nerves, focusing him on the start of the mission.

Now traveling at nearly a hundred-twenty knots, Professor deploys his wingsuit. The fabric between his legs and under his arms will allow him to fly to his destination.

Reaper Two-Six
Year 6

For a moment, he permits himself the pleasure of admiring the view from more than forty thousand feet. At four in the morning, the slight curvature of the Earth glistens along the horizon, showing just how small the atmosphere is, compared to space and the surface of the planet. Like embryonic fluid surrounding an unborn baby, the atmosphere breathes life into the Earth, while the blackness of space threatens to swallow the air, ending life as it is now. An amazing and fragile balance of universal forces keeps the beauty of life flowing.

He wonders, *Might evil finally be overcome if everyone is allowed to experience the fullness, perfection and splendor of the view from here? How can one not appreciate the immense, interconnected world that we call home?*

Enough, he snaps as his eyes bring into focus the Google glasses' head-up-display (HUD).

The custom GPS system provides a three-dimensional color display of the terrain below overlaid with critical navigational information: altitude, descent rate, airspeed, time, flight path and distance to the target zone. The image looks similar to a miniaturized aircraft primary flight screen projected onto the outer edge of a contact lens.

The experience is a bit disorienting at first, but the clarity and detail of the imagery provides the user with a beautiful vision of the ground for five miles in all directions.

Incredible, Professor sighs to himself, *I can easily identify individual mountain peaks, roads, vehicles and buildings.*

He twists, turns and rotates his body to get on course. The projected flight path in his HUD is represented by a series of rectangular boxes to fly through, very similar to modern aircraft navigational equipment. A quick check in the upper left hand corner of his HUD indicates the expected flight time remaining before touchdown, just under ten minutes.

Too bad, he thinks, *I could set a new world record for the longest flight in a wingsuit. I might have to talk Guinness into using telemetry data from my Android GPS system, but it would be worth it.* He chuckles under his breath.

He shakes images of an award from his mind because he knows he has only one shot at landing undetected in the proper location.

He keeps his body arched in order to maintain the proper pitch angle. Under ideal conditions, this provides the best glide ratio, allowing him to travel the farthest horizontal distance over the ground. The challenge is keeping his body fairly still in an unnatural position, with fully extended arms and legs for nearly ten minutes, all the while buffeted by nearly ninety knot winds.

"I'm going to need a chiropractor after tonight," he mumbles, trying to think of anything but the pain shooting down the backs of his legs and spine.

Back on the 727, Doc watches the timer in her helmet countdown, loosening her grip on the handhold. She checks her HUD to ensure it's functioning properly, preparing herself to jump. A moonless night over southern Nevada and miles from any real civilization, the sky looks like a gigantic black well. As the timer ticks to zero, Doc runs full tilt down the stairway and leaps out into nothingness.

Her life as she knows it … is changed forever.

Chapter 2
On a Wing and a Prayer

Whoosh! The sound of the wind is deafening inside Professor's helmet as he plummets down into the lower levels of the atmosphere. Even with the insulation of his wingsuit, he begins to feel the effects of the subzero temperature typically present above twenty-four thousand feet. Professor checks his HUD and verifies what the chill in his extremities have already told him: the temperature is a frigid twenty-eight degrees below zero Fahrenheit (thirty-three degrees below zero Centigrade).

Just the added challenge of trying not to shiver makes the task of maintaining the best glide path nearly impossible. If he drops too fast or too slowly, he'll miss his landing zone completely. He tries to ignore the aches in his arms, back and upper legs, keeping his body rigid and his focus on the HUD's speed indicator.

"Seventy, seventy, seventy," he mutters as he flies at exactly seventy knots toward the surface of the earth. If he keeps up this speed, he'll be over the landing zone in three minutes, perfect.

Professor sings the Steve Miller song *Fly Like An Eagle*, one of his favorite oldies, as he tries to block out the painful cramps trying to twist his body into knots.

Damn, he thinks, *I'm only forty-one years old. Shit, you'd think I was sixty as bad as I'm hurting.*

The training he and Doc went through over the last several months now seems like a holiday compared to his current agony. He can't imagine why this jump should be any different, except for the added stress that an actual mission incurs.

He shakes his head and blinks hard twice to clear his eyes; then he adjusts his arm positions slightly to sharpen his descent.

To minimize detection, all electromagnetic emissions were eliminated on their wingsuits, with just a passive GPS antenna for guidance. He wonders if Doc is okay. *Did she jump safely and on time? Is she able to follow the flight path to the targeted landing zone? Has their abandoned aircraft caused suspicion yet?*

Professor and Doc have a similar mindset at this moment, because both of them know that moving around undetected is their only chance for a successful mission. Should the take off, the flight, the jump, or the crash attract more attention than they expect, then the mission will be over before it begins.

On non-flying nights like tonight, only a skeleton crew, mostly security, is present at the flight test center. More commonly known as Area 51, the test center is located approximately eighty miles north-northwest of Las Vegas.

Area 51 is home to the United States' secret black ops projects, including weapons systems and experimental aircraft. The now famous SR-71 Blackbird, a long-range highly advanced Mach 3+ reconnaissance aircraft, first flew at Area 51 in the early 1960s. After serving the Air Force for more than thirty years, the SR-71 was eventually replaced by a significantly more advanced aircraft - the Aurora.

The one and a half by three-mile active region of Area 51 has more than a dozen large hangers and research buildings sprinkled over the western-most section, along with two main runways on the eastern side, the longest spanning twelve thousand feet. In addition, four more runways are located on the eleven square-mile Groom Lake salt flats, just north of the main complex.

Nearly surrounded on all sides by six- to nine thousand foot mountain peaks, Area 51 is nestled neatly in a desert basin. The location is ideal for carrying out covert research and development of advanced military technology.

With his helmet-mounted night vision system, Professor continues to scan the ground for any signs of activity. As most of the security is focused on keeping people from entering the base perimeter, which extends more than twelve miles in every direction from the main facility buildings, he anticipates minimal presence this close to the buildings.

No one should make it this far onto the base, he muses with a grin. *That's our ace-in-the-hole.*

The fact he is already well inside the parameter and now less than a minute from his intended landing zone is due to the thorough planning and execution of the mission details, something at which the Reapers excel.

Careful, he reminds himself, *this is the easy part of the mission.*

Flying dangerously close to the mountains, he begins the final approach turn, arching slightly while twisting his legs and shoulders. Grinding his teeth through the pain, he banks 180 degrees, rolling out with the landing zone now in full view.

Once I pull the chute, I'm dead if anyone spots me, he thinks. His heart rate begins to rise dramatically, and he continues to scan the ground. Professor slowly swings his head left and right then forward and rearward: *All clear.*

Reaper Two-Six
Year 6

A yellow light in his HUD suddenly begins to flash, indicating that he is less than five hundred feet from the ground. Five seconds later, he executes his parachute deployment procedure with pinpoint precision.

He brings his legs together and slightly arches his back. Carefully, he pulls both arms in alongside his body. Reaching back, he quickly deploys the pilot chute. Then, once again, he closes his arms, tucking them next to his side. The fully inflated pilot chute yanks out and releases the main canopy while Professor maintains as straight a posture with his arms, legs and back as possible.

One … two … three seconds pass.

Shoop!! The canopy fully deploys, yanking his harness tight and slowing his descent immediately.

Whew! he thinks while exhaling. He finally allows his lower body to relax for a few seconds now that the main chute has inflated.

He reaches up and grabs the steering toggles, checking the chute risers too. He then refocuses his attention to the ground, furiously scanning the area next to a hanger while holding his handgun ready.

Thank God, he thinks, *no one in sight.*

He thinks about Doc and hopes she is dealing with the jump better than he did. She's not much younger than he is, but she's in better shape. *Much better shape*, he chuckles silently.

He lightly touches down next to the side of the hanger and quickly gathers up the parachute. He then unzips and steps out of the wingsuit. He stuffs the chute into the body of the wingsuit and zips it closed. For the moment, he secures everything to his back, tying it off around his waist.

It's not very heavy, he thinks, *just a bit awkward*.

The plan is to take it with him, thereby not leaving any trace of his presence. However, should a scuffle, or worse a gun battle, break out, he's willing to ditch the chute and suit to insure the success of the mission.

Crawling along the ground, he makes his way to side door. Reaching into his pocket, he pulls out an electronic diaphragm, similar to what you'd see connected on the patient end of a stethoscope. He plugs one end into his helmet audio port, then rests the diaphragm against the hanger's metal wall.

Patiently, he listens and waits, while the acoustic software analyzes the audio data. He can feel the beating of his heart pulsating throughout his body, seemingly echoing in his ears. A full minute passes before a soft green light glows in his HUD.

No one's home, he thinks as he slowly rises to his feet. He swallows hard and pauses for just a second, before testing the door handle.

He smiles briefly to himself as the handle turns with his hand.

I knew it, he chuckles, w*hy lock the doors when you're not expecting any unwelcome visitors? Not like back home in Miami, that's for sure.* He shakes his head as he thinks about home. *Nope, at home there are bars on the windows and pet alligators serve as watchdogs.*

He slips inside the hanger and out of sight, gently closing the door behind him.

In the meantime, Doc is having a more difficult time with her jump. She doesn't know exactly what happened, but she is experiencing significantly increased drag and even intermittent flutter and control issues.

I could have a tear in the rear wing, she considers, *or a zipper that's come undone. Hell, for all I know, it's a zipper pull sticking out too far. Anything can cause too much drag at this speed and altitude. Nevertheless,* she snaps, trying to focus, *failure is not an option.*

She must keep her speed around a hundred knots to prevent spinning out of control. While this pushes her ahead of schedule, time wise, it also increases her sink rate dramatically. Her glide path has suffered, and she is falling on the lower side of the projected flight path, which means she may or may not be a viable member of this mission if she can't get to Professor's location.

The extra speed also makes it that much more difficult to maintain the proper posture because of the increased aerodynamic forces on her body. With the instability issues she's experiencing, each leg and arm has to be precisely positioned or it's game over.

"Four minutes," she grinds out from between her teeth, almost wishing she could have stayed back on the aircraft. The burning sensation radiating from her shoulders is immensely distracting and painful.

She enters the winding turns through the mountain pass when all of a sudden, "Shit!" she exclaims. "That was close!" She'd nearly sent herself into a flat spin.

The aerodynamic instability of her suit is worsening. She must continually increase her forward speed in order to maintain controllable flight. Consequently, her descent rate is rapidly increasing.

I aced the training runs with Professor, beating him in terms of flight path accuracy and time every single jump.

He was starting to get pissed, she remembers with a grim smile.

Now, with the mission on the line … she shakes her head in annoyance and frustration, realizing she must find an alternative landing site.

Her heart suddenly leaps into her throat as she spots a vehicle racing along a side road, the dust from its tires swirling into the air directly into her intended flight path. They are about to cross paths, with Doc less than a thousand feet from the ground.

She can't make any sudden turns with the condition of her suit, so she holds straight; hoping the altitude and moonless night will keep her disguised.

She inadvertently holds her breath until the vehicle races past without as much as a flash of the brake lights, allowing Doc to breathe a sigh of relief. She feels a bead of sweat drip down from behind her ear and onto her neck. She shivers, thinking how close that was.

Finalizing her plans to touchdown next to what looks like a dormitory, she begins the landing sequence. The dorm building is a good two thousand yards from her intended target zone and Professor, but she doesn't have a choice. She'll just have to try to make up time once she's on the ground.

Reaper Two-Six
Year 6

"Professor," she exclaims quietly, realizing the vehicle is now on a direct course toward his position.

She helplessly follows the vehicle with her eyes for a few seconds, hoping it veers away or Professor hears its approach. As she watches, the light in her HUD begins flashing yellow.

She wonders whether he landed safely and at the right location. *Was he detected? Has he located the aircraft? Will I be able to get to him without being noticed?*

When the light in her HUD begins flashing red, Doc knows she can't worry about Professor now. With less than three hundred feet before her own landing, she has to make precision movements that demand her attention. Once on the ground, she'll worry.

Without hesitation, she throws the pilot chute and positions her body for the main canopy deployment. The ground is now rushes up toward her at an astounding rate. Finally, she hears a *shoop!* as the main chute inflates.

Instinctively, she realizes that a hard landing is imminent, as the main canopy didn't have time to slow her descent enough.

Quickly and with focus, she places her feet and knees together, ensuring her legs are slightly bent. With her toes pointed, the balls of her feet are the first to contact the ground. Immediately, she sharply twists and bends her body to the right. She continues to fall onto her side, hitting her upper leg, thigh, buttocks and finally, her shoulder.

"OOF!"

The vocalization is unintended, but forced from her lungs as she rolls onto her back with a thud.

Without warning, the still partially inflated chute begins to drag her across the hard packed desert ground "Whoa, whoa, whoa," she half whispers, half yells.

She reaches out, grabs the risers and pulls with all her strength, trying to collapse the chute. Tumbling across the ground, she finally smacks into the side of the dormitory with a deadening *THWACK!* Then, as if to add insult to injury, the collapsed chute drapes over her as if she's dead and it is her shroud.

"Son of a bitch," she mutters. "That landing could have gone a bit smoother."

She pulls at the nylon frantically, trying to find an edge to the monstrous canopy so she can roll it up. Realizing her landing was a lot louder than planned, she gathers her chute and just sits on the ground against the wall, handgun ready… her heart racing and her mouth dry. She scans the immediate vicinity with her helmet's night vision system until she is satisfied that she hasn't raised an alarm. After several long moments, she begins to relax.

She shakes her head and grins thinking, *Damn, Professor, you were right. This place is practically deserted. Who'd have thought that a top-secret military installation would be a ghost town?*

Finally feeling comfortable enough to move, Doc steps out of her wingsuit and stuffs her chute back into the center, zipping it up securely. Her HUD still has the original landing location in its memory, so she begins to make her way to her intended target on the other side of the base, hoping to meet up with Professor.

Chapter 3
Ghosts in the Dark

Screech! The Jeep skids to a stop outside the Aurora's hanger. Two men get out, slamming the doors shut behind them.

"Yes sir, yes sir," Mason says, speaking briskly into his cell phone.

He reaches out and quickly opens the hanger's side door, listening to the CO's final instructions. Mason throws a glare at Dillon, the other MP, while motioning his arm and pointing inside the hanger.

"On it, sir," Mason says, snapping his phone closed. "Christ!" he mutters as he steps into the cool darkness of the hanger. He flips on the overhead lights as the door slams shut behind him.

As an Air Force MP with more than nine years under his belt, Mason's dependable service and tactful methods have put him in the good graces of many top officials, including some in the Office of Special Investigations (AFOSI).

This division of the Air Force is heavily involved in protection of critical technologies, threat mitigation, and numerous other specialized investigative services. His aspiration to be a Special Agent for the AFOSI is the only reason he'd taken this post for the past two years in the middle of nowhere Nevada.

Because the AFOSI is considered an elite division, posts within it are highly sought out. Mason hopes his current top secret experience will give him an advantage during the next round of Special Agent applications.

"What's the urgency?" Dillon barks at Mason.

"Top brass are heading our way. Some sort of high tech show and tell I guess," replies Mason. "The CO wants everything spiffy before 0600. So, we have to clean the area and wash the Aurora."

"You're shitting me, right? Wash that beast?" Dillon says, pointing at the aircraft with a look of disgust and disbelief on his face.

Mason ignores his partner and goes about the business of straightening up the general hanger area. He pulls the weapons cart back into its proper storage location marked on the floor. The awful wheel *squeak, squeak* rips down his spine. He shutters almost uncontrollably as the unpleasant sound resonates through his ear canal, jolting his entire body.

"Jesus!" he grumbles loudly. "Do you see any spray oil over there?"

Dillon stops organizing the back wall of shelves and turns around, holding a can over his head. "Here you go," he calls back. Dillon throws the can in a football spiral.

Mason grabs it in a perfect catch. "Nice toss. Thanks!" he says.

"Welcome," Dillon responds while turning back to his task of straightening the disorganized equipment and jumbled paperwork on the back wall shelving.

He places checklists onto clipboards and hangs them up. "Pilots," he says. "You'd think they owned the freaking place. They're too good to even put away their checklists."

He finishes the last clipboard and proceeds to gather the notes from the previous day and other mission sensitive paperwork, strewn haphazardly around the table.

"Let's see," he says, putting pages into the appropriately labeled folders. "Weapons ... fuel ... instruments ... oxygen ... engine ... navigation ... brakes ... radar ... space."

"These brainy dudes," he adds, shaking his head and muttering under his breath. "And my mom thought I was messy."

Mason finishes pushing the fuel and pylon loading assist carts into their respective storage areas, finally clearing a path in front of the aircraft.

Reaper Two-Six
Year 6

*We might as well get started washing the Aurora,
since it's probably going to take us at least a half hour,* he
thinks. *It should easily dry by 0600.*

In order to spray off the aircraft, they need to tow it
out of the hanger. Mason walks to the side wall and presses
the OPEN button. The huge doors creak and groan as they
start to separate, allowing the hanger light to break the
blackness of the early morning sky. Once the doors are
sufficiently open for the wingspan, he smacks the STOP
button. Squeaking and shaking, the thirty-foot tall doors
grind to a halt.

Grabbing the ground tow bar, he drags it toward the
nose wheel. With a swift action, he snaps it into place,
securing it with a pin.

Walking over to the ground-handling tractor, Mason
motions to Dillon. Still unhappy about being treated like a
classified maid service, Dillon heads for the hanger's far
corner.

We're going to do this the easy way, he thinks as he
heads over to the fire hose. "Hey Mason, what do you
think?" he yells across the hanger.

Mason sees Dillon drumming his fingers on the fire
hose reel and grins. "Looks like a solid idea to me."

Mason steps into the cab of the electric powered tractor, turns it on, and drives it out onto the tarmac. Whipping a full U-turn, he lines up with the boom.

Slowly, slowly, he mutters. The solid *ka-chunk* brings a smile to his face as the boom slides onto the tractor's front mounted hitch.

Flipping open the door, he jumps down and secures a pin into the boom. He stretches, looking around the corner of the aircraft, but doesn't see any evidence of Dillon.

Clown, he thinks, hopping back into the tractor's cab, *do I have to do everything around here?*

Carefully, he eases the aircraft out of the hanger, marveling at how the Aurora's fuselage blends into the dark morning sky. It's covered in non-reflective black ceramic tiles, similar to those used on the Space Shuttle. *It's like this aircraft doesn't exist*, he thinks, smirking. *Like it's a black hole; light and energy hit the craft's surface, but none of it reflects.*

The Aurora's sharp triangular-shaped delta fuselage extends more than one hundred feet and ends in a wingspan of more than sixty feet. The razor thin highly-swept twin vertical tails are more than twenty feet long and are located symmetrically outboard, near the rear of the Aurora. The knife-like trailing edges of the main fuselage and vertical tails abruptly end at the rear of the aircraft.

The tubular looking center section of the fuselage houses the pilot and rear seat navigation officer stations. Smoothly contoured, the Aurora's bulbous middle gracefully tapers rearward, essentially vanishing into the fuselage about three-quarters of the way back.

The engine system is tightly packed into the aircraft's underside. Aft of the cockpit, a complex set of air inlets are imbedded into the wedge-shaped underbelly. The on-board digital engine controller monitors dozens of flight characteristics, while continuously adjusting numerous vanes in the engine air inlet system. During hypersonic flight, one misaligned vane could easily cause a massive engine stall, sending the Aurora into an unrecoverable flat spin.

The impressive seventy-plus-ton aircraft sits delicately perched on a pair of short stalky-looking main landing gear. Supported by four wheels, each of the gear's structural columns extend upward, anchored to the Aurora's fuselage adjacent to either side of the engine bay. A standard military style nose landing gear system supports the forward section of the long aircraft.

After shutting off the tractor, Mason checks his watch, 04:48. With Dillon nowhere to be seen, Mason decides to take a ten-minute smoke break. *Might as well,* he thinks. *Nothing to do until Dillon decides to join me with the hose.*

He walks casually away from the aircraft, nearly to the center of the main taxiway. Looking skyward, he admires the beauty and vastness of the sky and stars.

Reaching into his pocket, he plucks a cigarette, flicks his lighter, and takes a deep draw. After a few seconds, he exhales and nods his head in a soothing agreement.

"Nice," is all he manages as he starts to relax, the nicotine coursing its way throughout his body. The orange glow of the cigarette tip partially illuminates his face.

Professor has been patiently waiting in hiding along the darkened hanger's sidewall, listening with his electronic diaphragm. The time has come to act. Darting out from the blackness, he slips under the Aurora, and sneaks his way to the front of the aircraft. Pausing for a moment behind the tractor to recheck the position of both MPs, Professor sets his plan into motion.

He slinks around the side of the tractor's cab and approaches the MP's slightly-illuminated shoulders. With a swift, accurate motion, he grabs Mason from behind, securing him in a sleeper hold.

Within seconds, Mason is limp and unconscious.
Professor drags him to the side of the hanger and injects him
with a general anesthetic. *That'll keep him out for a while.*
I'll be long gone by the time he wakes up, Professor thinks.

Keenly aware that the other MP still lurks somewhere
in the hanger, Professor utilizes his infrared HUD system. He
scans slowly, until two strong heat sources become clear at
the far-side of the Aurora's hanger; one seemingly sitting on
the floor and the other walking in his general direction.

Doc, is that you? he wonders as he unholsters his
handgun and backs off to a more secluded location. Until he
is sure, the approaching person is a target.

Still too far away to see detailed features; his heart
rate begins to rise, while sweat develops on his forehead. The
seconds tick away with the sound of the person's footsteps,
as soft as they are, still pounding in his helmet's audio
system.

He watches as the person breaks through the unseen
barrier of the hanger doorway, heading toward the aircraft.
Bending slightly, the person walks under the left wing,
passing next to the main gear assembly. Extending a right
arm, the person reaches out and slides their right hand
alongside the engine bay, almost as if admiring the smooth
texture of the Aurora's skin.

Continuing forward, following the inlet system and the cockpit underbelly, the person stops at the front wheel assembly. Bending down, the person unhooks the tow bar, then scans the area.

A smile brightens his features as he watches the shapely figure and familiar movements of his fellow Reaper.

It is Doc. You can't do as much training together as we have without becoming super sensitive to each other's mannerisms.

Still, he feels a rush of relief to know she made it down safely. He rises to join her when he sees her wave him to approach. No words need to be spoken; they just bump knuckles upon greeting. *There will be time enough to catch up later, once we are long gone from this place,* he tells himself, even though he really wants to know how her jump went.

Doc opens the Aurora's canopy and climbs up the fuselage footholds. She settles into the pilot seat, stuffing the chute and wingsuit next to her. After a few flips and button pushes, the electronics glow to life.

"Full tank," she calls to Professor.

That's music to my ears, Professor thinks as he drives the tow tractor away from the front of the aircraft.

Reaper Two-Six
Year 6

Doc pulls out her Android Smartphone, clicks in the micro USB plug, then scans the panel. A few seconds later, "Ah," she whispers, and plugs the other end of the cord into the navigation system.

After swiping her phone, entering the password, she activates the FTP program.

"Downloading," she says.

Professor peels off the engine inlet and exhaust covers, tossing them into the hanger. He notices the light orange glow of the impending sunrise beginning to illuminate the horizon. *We better get out of here*, he thinks, *those damn MPs put us more than forty minutes behind schedule.*

He walks out in front of the aircraft, turns toward the cockpit, and whirls his right hand in the air, making a circular motion with his index finger.

He swallows hard. *This is it*, he thinks, as the engines roar to life, *from here on out, our presence is no secret.*

Chapter 4
First Light

Colonel Landis exits his personal quarters and heads toward the jeep that will carry him to his 'crack of dawn' meeting. As he angrily strides down the sidewalk, he checks his security detail at the same time to insure they are all at their posts.

While riding to the main HQ building, he reflects on the phone call that woke him from his sleep at 0400 hours. He didn't mind interrupted sleep for emergencies, but calls from his superior's assistant announcing that the scheduled meeting had suddenly been moved from 1000 to 0500 was too much for the Colonel's sensibilities. In fact, he barely had time to wash-up and gulp down a cup of coffee.

For the past four years, Colonel Landis has served as the CO of Area 51. Landis is the stereotypical Air Force Colonel — fit and well-toned, even at fifty-nine years of age. His chiseled features and strong face project the intensity of his presence, along with his piercing blue-green eyes that miss nothing.

As usual, he dresses in his uniform of pants with a razor crease, shirt and tie. He radiates professionalism, even today, as he frantically rushed to get dressed to meet his guests by 0500.

"Crazy," he snarls. "We can have a meeting at a more civilized hour and still accomplish as much."

"Damn boondoggle this is going to be anyway," he growls in frustration. "Fiscal concerns my ass! This is a top-secret facility; we are exempt from fiscal responsibility. If we have to ask for fund appropriations every time we used a square of toilet paper to wipe our asses, this place would stink to high heaven. They're all just a bunch of bureaucratic assholes."

The jeep makes a wide turn around the side of the HQ building and pulls into the Colonel's reserved spot. He jumps out of the vehicle and strides toward the main entrance doors, still grumbling under his breath about the annoying last minute rescheduling.

Before the Colonel can set one foot inside the building, a black limo swings into the front circle drive and pulls up near him, screeching to a halt. The driver gets out and proceeds to open both rear doors for the occupants to exit.

"Sir!" Colonel Landis says as he snaps a smart salute.

Mr. Dow, the Secretary of the Air Force, and Mr. Mallory, the Secretary of Defense, both return the greeting and then enter the base's main HQ building. Sneering, Colonel Landis follows close behind.

The base is located in a dry, desolate area. As a consequence, sounds travel quite well, at least near to the ground.

As the MPs close the doors behind Colonel Landis, a light rumbling is suddenly apparent. While walking through the main lobby, Secretary Dow says, "A bit early for testing, isn't it?"

"Sir, we are always testing something. Got to keep your flyboys happy, Mr. Secretary," the Colonel lies, quickly motioning to one of the MPs. "Excuse me for just a moment, gentlemen. Please help yourselves to the pastries and coffee. I won't be long."

"Get on the horn and find out what the hell is going on. I was quite clear that all testing was to cease by 2300 last night. Everything is to be spotless for this morning's guests. I want the testing stopped immediately. Do whatever you have to. Understand?"

"Yes sir!" the MP responds, offering a salute. The Colonel returns the salute and immediately the MP turns away to race out the door.

The MP crosses the courtyard and enters a small security building. He quickly checks the duty roster and frantically starts making phone calls.

The rumbling turns into a roar, continuing to increase in volume. About ready to explode in anger, the Colonel punches through the front doors, looking for the MP. Now, the intensity of the roar, combined with the reverberation off the surrounding mountains, has increased dramatically, leaving little doubt as to the source of the rumble.

"Wait a second ..." is all the Colonel can muster while slowing turning his head. At that precise instant, he looks toward the source of the roar and sees the Aurora lift off the runway.

At the same time, both secretaries join him in the front lot. All three men stare, dumbfounded, as the aircraft rapidly ascends into the clear morning sky. Aside from the diminishing roar of the engines, there is silence until the MP bursts through the door of the guardhouse.

"Colonel, it's the Aurora. I, uh, I mean, we believe the aircraft has taken off."

The Colonel turns a steely gaze on the MP. "Really? That's very observant of you, considering the fact that it just flew past our fucking faces. Who took her without my authorization?"

Reaper Two-Six
Year 6

"I'm sorry sir, but all test pilots are accounted for."

"Meaning what?" The Colonel is now mere inches from the MP, a fierce scowl on his face.

"Uh, I, sorry, I mean, we think it was stolen … sir." The MP can see the end of his career staring at him through the Colonel's eyes.

"Stolen?" The Colonel smiles, but it isn't a smile that conveys happiness. It's more of a smile that means someone's nuts are in a vise and the Colonel has the crank in his hand. And he is getting more furious by the second.

"Yes sir, stolen."

"Bullshit, that's impossible. Only authorized personnel are on this base. I'll guarantee it's some itchy-fingered flyboy who couldn't wait to get that bird in the air and is going for a joy ride. If so, that means someone is covering for him. So I suggest you get your ass down to the hanger — *now!* Report back to me ASAP with a name."

"Yes sir."

"One more thing," the Colonel adds, "Call Nellis Air Force Base. Have them scramble a few birds to investigate."

"But, sir, won't that —"

"I said call Nellis, soldier. Is that a problem for you?"

The MP shakes his head furiously, "No sir. I'll get on it right away, sir."

Reaper Two-Six
Year 6

In the Aurora's cockpit, Doc keeps the throttle wide open to gain altitude and distance as fast as possible; but this leaves them vulnerable to tracking equipment. It's a risk they have to take in order for the mission to succeed.

"I've got our back." Professor says over the comm from the rear seat. "Electronics are active."

As an electronics expert in the United States Navy, Professor originally settled on a military career as an F-14D back-seater, the radio intercept officer (RIO). After four years, he earned his pilot's license and served another nine years before leaving the Navy. As a combination pilot/RIO, the Reapers immediately snatched him up to be a member of their elite squadron.

Nodding in acknowledgement, Doc continues to scan her instruments, still getting used to the immense power of the aircraft. "She sure is a pocket rocket. I haven't flown anything this fast since my X-plane days."

"Contact," Professor interrupts. "Eight birds southeast about seventy miles, probably F-15s and 16s out of Nellis."

"Roger." Doc acknowledges. "Passing forty-five thousand feet on a southwest heading. This baby sure can move."

The planned course will take them over southern California, just north of Los Angeles and then out over the Pacific. Eventually, they'll turn south and upload a new set of coordinates for their final destination.

"Once we hit sixty-thousand feet, I'll pull her back and level off at two-thousand knots." Doc informs. "That'll allow us to be in full stealth mode, hopefully keeping our Nellis boys from tracking us."

Professor continues to watch the eight bogies as they close in, now less than thirty miles away. "Come on, Doc," he whispers. *They're still pretty far away* ... "Oh shit!"

"How many?" Doc asks, maintaining her intense focus on the cockpit instruments.

After a long pause that feels like hours, Professor finally blurts out, a bit startled, "Twelve." He was prepared for a battle, but even this took him by surprise. In all his years, he's never seen twelve missiles in the air at the same time, and never tracking just one target.

"Guess they figured we aren't on a joy ride," Doc says, adding a chuckle to help calm her nerves.

"And they're willing to destroy their only working model for fear of it getting into the wrong hands," Professor adds.

"How long do we have before impact?" Doc asks.

"Sixty-five seconds."

"Heat-seekers?" Doc asks.

"Doubtful, probably Sparrows. It's a long shot for seekers. But we'd better assume both. We only have one chance to survive this."

After a few seconds of intense thought, Doc asks, "High-low with flares and ECM?"

Professor scans all the screens. *Twelve*, he reminds himself, shaking his head in amazement. *The good thing is they're all close together, following nearly identical flight paths.*

After a few more seconds assimilating all the data available to him, he finally pipes up, "Yes. I'll give you the count."

"Ready."

Doc increases her grip on both the stick and throttle; this maneuver will jar the aircraft as well as its two occupants.

The seconds tick away in silence. Doc and Professor are a masterful image of concentration and teamwork.

"3 ... 2 ... 1 ... Now!" he calls out.

Doc rolls the aircraft 180 degrees and quickly pulls back on the stick. Once stable in a steep dive, she punches into full afterburner. Nearly four g's force Doc and Professor into their seats, their heads pinned against the rests. She rolls the aircraft another 180 degrees and continues to accelerate in the dive.

Professor activates the ECM system and prepares to fire the flares, watching the screens for the right moment.

"Whoa," he says as the twelve missiles home in on them, now less than a thousand yards away. *"Now!"*

Doc chops the throttle and pulls back on the stick as hard as she can. The plane violently pitches upward, partially in a tail skid.

At the same time, Professor releases the flares. Showering streams of glowing embers pop from the aircraft's tail section.

"Ugh" is the only sound either of them manages as the g forces from the aircraft's maneuvers push them even deeper into their seats.

Doc eyes the attitude indicator, and at the critical moment, pushes the throttle to full afterburner again. The plane lurches forward, climbing out of the dive, rapidly gaining altitude.

The missiles scream past, narrowly missing the tail section of the Aurora.

Doc lets out a heavy breath, and says, "Guess it worked. We're still here. But that was close."

Reaper Two-Six
Year 6

Rapidly scanning the instruments, Professor concludes, "All clear."

"What if we head south now and enter stealth mode? Those fighters will be hard pressed to track us and our current altitude of forty-two thousand feet should provide enough margin for me to evaluate any new encounters," he adds.

Doc nods in agreement. She levels the Aurora's altitude, accelerates to just over two-thousand knots, then turns south.

As if going into a black hole, the aircraft effectively vanishes from the world. Nothing remains but a tiny, insignificant dot ripping through the sky.

Chapter 5
A Question of Worthiness

"How much longer before we reach our destination?" Professor asks over the comm. As he waits for an answer, he scans the scopes, looking for signs that their stealth mode is working properly. *All clear,* he concludes, and nods in relief.

"About an hour from now," Doc replies, her voice quavering slightly with emotion. "Then if you're up for a power descent, it'll take another five minutes to get directly over the camp."

Professor can't help but notice the anxiety in her voice. He knows that her concern for the success of the mission is growing, but bringing those concerns to light won't change the course they set in motion.

Doc knows that she isn't masking her feelings very well, but she can't help it. She can't believe she went along with the mission on Professor's terms. Now she feels the added strain of doubt… doubt that they did the right thing… doubt that they'll be convincing enough to RAFCO to make them believe that they've really switched sides… and doubt that the terrorists need them enough to keep them alive once they've turned the Aurora over to them.

Oh my God, she thinks, *what are we doing? Do we really think we can pull this off?*

Along with the fear of bringing shame upon her family, other doubts race through her mind. *We should have contacted PVL before taking the Aurora,* she reflects. *Damn it Professor, I can't believe you talked me into this. Even if we turn around, returning the Aurora to Area 51, the government will still convict us of treason. There is no escaping the fact that our lives are over now.*

Professor realizes that he'd better talk to Doc and try to calm her down and alleviate whatever concerns she has before they get to the RAFCO base.

"What's up, Doc?" he asks in a cheerful attempt to lighten the mood. This phrase never failed to garner a smile in the past, because it reminded her of her favorite cartoon character, Bugs Bunny.

This time it doesn't work. Doc's nervousness runs deeper this time, and although she can appreciate Professor's attempt to cheer her up, she can't overcome the dark thoughts that cloud her mind.

"Do you really believe they aren't going to kill us as soon as we land in El Charco?" she asks, and then adds, "I mean seriously, they'll have the aircraft, so why keep us alive?"

Reaper Two-Six
Year 6

"Doc, listen to me." Professor's voice softly echoes through the aircraft's comm system. "We both know one thing with absolute certainty — they need us. No one at RAFCO knows enough about the Aurora to even start the engines, much less how to use the hypersonic stealth mode or any of the enhanced weapons' features. So they need us for whatever they're planning."

"That's another point. What are they planning? We can't be sure that they only want to use it in a public spectacle of some kind, like blowing it up near U.S. soil, or just off the coast somewhere. Hell, for all we know, they want to use us as part of that display, you know, the rogue pilots who hate America so much they've switched sides. If that's the case, then we're going to ruin our lives for nothing."

"No, Doc, I don't agree with you," Professor says softly. "Embarrassing their enemy has never been RAFCO's agenda or motive in the past. They always aim much higher than that."

"I know, but…"

"But nothing. RAFCO is planning something much bigger. I can feel it in my bones. We just didn't have time to gather enough detailed intelligence before they sprang this mission on us. It's not like we could've said no. We'd have blown our cover then. We had no choice but to go along with them." The last part was a little harsh, and he hopes he hasn't gone too far and pushed her further into doubt.

Pausing, he glances forward and sees Doc's silky soft raven-colored hair flowing out from under her pilot's helmet and around the sides of her seat. Sighing, he realizes the forcefulness of his tone isn't necessary. She's not questioning their decision, but instead their ability to complete the real mission — infiltrate RAFCO and bring them down.

"I know in your heart, Doc, you believe in what we're doing."

He sees her nod silently in agreement.

"You know I do," Doc says. "I dedicated over five years of my life to the Reapers. I just have a hard time believing it's over. I just can't believe all that bullshit the politicians' fed the global community so they'd stop funding the GDO. Unreal."

"Fucking homeland security bastards," he snarls. "I never thought Wolverine would bow to them like he did, but what choice did he have after the assassination of NATO+'s president? It took the spark out of him."

"Hell, it wasn't just Wolverine, it was Loz too." Doc says.

Doc takes her eyes off the console for a few seconds, her mind straying to the painful events of just under a year ago. What had happened so drastically to put her in this predicament? She could never have seen how different her life was going to turn out if she had gone to a fortune teller. Her life had done a 180-degree turn, and she'd had little to no warning.

The sketchy details she was able to piece together included a Hollywood style breach in the GDO's computer system. That breach resulted in a trumped-up Homeland Security hearing, eventually forcing the commanders of the GDO to turn over sensitive data to the investigating authorities.

Thankfully, Vice Admiral PVL strategically selected the information released, which turned out to be enough to satisfy the authorities, but not enough to expose Reaper Two-Six. Unfortunately, that data was not enough to satisfy the self-serving Congressional committee members.

The political posturing that followed resulted in the resignation of Elena Filatov, the president of NATO+. Elena, a staunch supporter of the GDO, knew the real work of the Reapers, and the enormous contributions they made extinguishing global terrorism. Unfortunately, most of their work and success was secret in order to protect their identities.

In the three days following Elena Filatov's resignation, the Senate committee reached their decision: to permanently remove all GDO funding. With the United States' funding cut off, other nations quickly followed, cutting or completely eliminating their financial support for the GDO, forcing a complete shut down and closing of GDO operations.

In a final attempt to save the GDO, the three Reaper commanders — Wolverine, PVL and Loz — made an appeal for an audience with the entire NATO+ assembly. The commanders decided to reveal some of the successes of the Reapers over the past five years, and demonstrate how each country's small amount of funding had combined into one global organization, the GDO, whose sole mission was to fight terrorism. This one small, dedicated fierce group had a singular purpose of exterminating terrorism from the face of the earth, all the while remaining behind the scenes and basically unknown to the world.

Elena and Wolverine travelled to the NATO+ General Assembly Hall, discussing their plans for this final attempt to regain funding. Wolverine was hopeful that upon learning the true nature and full extent of the successes of the GDO and the Reapers, the members of NATO+ would continue or renew their support.

But a great tragedy struck, and their hopes were savagely crushed. While walking up to the podium, Elena was shot in the chest by a terrorist assassin. She fell dead at Wolverine's feet while a stunned body of world statesmen looked on in horror.

Elena's death was mourned heavily, the loss of a great evangelist for a safe world.

Since Elena's death occurred on U.S. soil, Homeland Security led the investigation and quickly concluded that it was orchestrated by the Continental Bolivarian Movement (CBM). Wolverine knew the truth: the CBM was really a front to confuse the authorities, hiding the real mastermind, RAFCO, from being discovered. Unfortunately, Wolverine's plea to the investigative team fell upon deaf ears, as the secretary had another agenda in mind.

In a performance worthy of an academy award, the Secretary of Homeland Security delivered a speech praising the local police, FBI and CIA for their swift apprehension of the gunman, and blaming a renegade anti-terrorist group for interfering with official police business. The secretary all but blamed the GDO for Elena's death.

The weeks following Elena's funeral saw an end to the Reapers. The GDO's three global command centers were shutdown. All the aircraft and computer equipment were moved to the Western GDO center in Australia and mothballed. The Reapers were painfully required to turn in their wings.

Through some talented negotiations by Loz, each Reaper received a year's pay and a secluded place to live, complements of Luo Chuan, the newly appointed Chinese Premier, whom the Reapers essentially placed in power.

Doc thought PVL was just angry. He seemed to be acting out of character and doing odd things. One day he asked them to turn in their wings, then a week later he requested them for this mission; a mission totally outside the authority of the Reapers and the GDO.

Suddenly, Doc's distracted thoughts snap back to the situation at hand. She carefully monitors the plane's activities while making sure there are no extraneous radar returns that need her attention.

"Hang on," she says. "Master warning on the number two engine fuel pre-heater."

She flips a few switches and cross-checks the engine's performance with other sensors. Her eyes dart around, quickly absorbing the associated data. In preparation, she snaps the two throttle control handles to the unlock position. This allows her manual control of each engine.

"You got anything?"

Professor cycles through screen menus, frantically trying to figure out if this is a bad sensor or a real situation.

"Pull 'er back five percent."

"Roger, five percent."

Carefully, she reduces the number two engine's power. To compensate, the yaw dampers increase to maintain straight flight.

They both scan their respective engine health screens. The maze of colored data tells the ominous story. The pre-heater appears to have stopped working.

"Can we bypass and use the number one only?" Doc asks. Her six years of piloting experimental aircraft is a benefit now, as the Aurora didn't come with a user's manual.

"Not sure, checking now," Professor says as he starts to pull up schematics on his LCD screen. He needs to know which valves he can control from within the cockpit.

"We've got only about five minutes before the engine flames out. You need me to go subsonic?"

If the temperature of the methane fuel mixture drops below its flash point, it will no longer burn. At hypersonic speeds, spinning out of control is a very real possibility if the thrust levels of the two engines are not carefully monitored and controlled.

With well over two minutes gone, he says at last, "Damn it, I guess we'd better. I've got an idea, but I'll need to reset the breaker."

"Roger, cutting the hypersonic engines."

Immediately, they are startled as the engine abruptly backfires, at least that's what it felt like.

"What in the hell was that?" Professor says, annoyed at the unexpected jarring that pulsated through the fuselage.

The fuel remaining in the main lines is still under pressure and at elevated temperatures. With the sudden closing of the lines, the overboard dump value popped open momentarily, releasing its combustible mixture. The heat from the skin caused it to detonate.

"Do what you're going to do and fast." Doc says, with an impending sense of doom tightening in her stomach. "We'd better not stick around here long. That noise could have exposed us."

For the moment, the aircraft coasts high above the eastern Pacific Ocean, due west of Mexico City. The aircraft, now passing through Mach 1.8, continues to decelerate rapidly. Doc increases nose trim to maintain altitude, awaiting the go ahead from Professor.

The back seat is a flurry of activity as Professor manipulates numerous buttons, switches and dials in an effort to stabilize the number two engine fuel temperature. Every so often he stops to watch a screen or two, making mental notes as the data flashes in front of him. A few moments later, the plane heaves and rolls as it settles into subsonic flight.

"I sure hope they fix that on next year's model." Doc says with a shaky laugh, as she wrestles with the controls. She knows that if they can't get the hypersonic engines back online, they'll have to continue the rest of the flight on conventional jet propulsion, increasing their flight time dramatically, and more importantly, exposing them to sensitive tracking equipment.

With the final switch combination complete, Professor says, "Give her a try."

The happy radiance of Doc's face says it all. *If only the comm system could transmit emotions*, she thinks. "Well done."

"Don't thank me yet, it's only a patch. I bypassed the temperature limits on the number one pre-heater. That'll give us a little more than fifty percent capability; I'm guessing sixty-five percent will be our maximum."

Doc tries to listen, but her focus is keeping the aircraft under control as it rapidly accelerates again. More instinctual than an actual acknowledgement, she says. "Roger."

"I'm climbing to seventy-five thousand feet. You know these babies like the cold, thin air anyway, and I want more distance with the ground to better insure our safety."

"Good idea. I'm back to watching our tail. The pre-heater seems stabilized; about five percent over red-line, but it should do us."

"Guess we'll be late. Should I phone ahead to make sure the porch light is still on?" Professor smirks, trying to lighten the mood.

The joke is lost on Doc, as the intense concentration of hypersonic piloting takes hold. As seconds lead to minutes, she begins to relax. They appear to be still in the clear.

Doc feels a small sense of relief and ponders their fate when they finally land on Colombian soil.

I guess Professor is right; they will *need us, now. As far as RAFCO is concerned, the Aurora is broken. If she is unable to maintain hypersonic stealth flight, they'll need us to help fix her. At least that's the story we need to stick by. That should hopefully buy us enough time to uncover what they're planning.*

She reaches over and calls up the moving map display. *Twenty-four minutes*, it reads. Nodding, she prepares herself to step back into the character known to RAFCO; the rogue pilot willing to do whatever it takes.

Chapter 6
The Hunt Begins

Area 51, southwestern Nevada, United States

"I heard you the first time," Colonel Landis says into the phone, slamming his fist on the desk. "No. I'll speak to them myself. You find me that bird."

Colonel Landis slams the phone down, hanging up on the Commander of Nellis Air Force base. His modest build and five-foot, seven-inch frame has never been mistaken for weakness due to his overbearing personality and gruff voice. In fact, when meeting the Colonel for the first time, the surprise is hard to suppress. At age fifty-nine, the Colonel's serious demeanor and extensive flight-testing background make him an ideal fit to take command of Area 51.

He releases the handset and sits back in his office chair. He reaches down and slides open the bottom desk drawer, where his bottle of nerve medicine lays buried behind a heavy-duty roster file.

"Hmmm," he mutters, "it's awful early."

He mulls over his schedule for a few moments before he makes his final decision; then he pours himself a shot and swiftly knocks it back. The smooth, thirty-year-old single malt scotch slides down his throat like a buttered ball of fire, warming his insides. He closes his eyes to the pleasure and sighs heavily.

Few things in life give him as much pleasure as a fine Scotch whiskey, but then again, few things can comfort him at times like this either.

With his eyes still closed, he slowly lowers his right arm and places the shot glass on the desk. He lets the warmth take over him as he savors the moment when the edge comes off his nerves. Now, he can face anything.

The knocking at the door snaps the Colonel out of his short daze. "Come in." he calls out.

The MP throws open the door and hands him a note pad. After a few moments of flipping pages, the Colonel raises his eyebrows and looks at the MP. He hands the notepad back to him.

"Bring me Mason and Dillon. I want to hear it from them directly. Also, get Felix in here. He should be arriving on the 0530 commuter from Vegas."

"Who sir?"

"Dr. Schroder."

"Oh. Yes sir. I'll speak to the operations guards and have him brought down as soon as he arrives."

The MP salutes, waits for the Colonel to respond, then disappears into the main lobby of the HQ building, finally exiting onto the front lot. He hops into a jeep, and floors it, dashing off to the hanger to pick up Mason and Dillon.

Alone again, the Colonel glances around the room, and reminisces about the sixty-plus year history of Area 51 depicted in pictures hanging on the walls of his office. Shaking his head in disbelief, he runs his fingers through his distinctive gray hair. It's no secret that his thirty-eight-year military career has seen a new first, the theft of a top-secret aircraft. Even with his extraordinary powers of persuasion, Colonel Landis knows that this particular piece of shit is going to stick to him, and it just might ruin his career no matter what he does.

Down the hall in the LeMay room, Secretaries Mallory and Dow await an update on the aircraft situation. Named in honor of the late General Curtis LeMay, Air Force Chief of Staff, the LeMay room operates as Area 51's official war room. All communications in or out of the base are monitored here. As needed, it also doubles as a conference room or operations center for base logistics.

Feeling the weight of the Air Force's reputation on his shoulders, the Colonel neatly dons his hat, then swipes the folder off the desk before exiting into the lobby. As he approaches the conference room, a loud voice becomes apparent. Peeking in, he sees Secretary Mallory on the phone with Secretary Dow, seemingly assisting him by flipping pages and taking notes in a book. Having known both secretaries for a few years, he decides it's best to wait elsewhere.

After making his way down the long hallway, he opens the front door and heads for the veranda. The remoteness of the facility demands that all personnel have access to relaxation and recreational options. When personnel are required to stay on base for days, weeks or longer, these facilities become therapeutic. Studies show that even the most dedicated workaholic needs a place to work out their frustrations or ponder life in a peaceful atmosphere. The veranda fulfills that need.

Basketball, occasional flag football, and a few other sports are often played late in the evening, once the heat of the midday subsides. There is also a covered area to sit at tables, with food available from the café. At this hour of the morning, it's actually a bit chilly, typical for the desert environment; but late afternoons and early evenings blaze with heat.

Ah, the cool air. The Colonel nods while walking along the backside of the building. After lighting a cigarette and enjoying a few puffs, he looks up at the last of the stars still twinkling before made invisible by the morning's sun.

He wonders about the stars he can't see now, that are normally visible at night.

The stars are still there, I just can't see them. He smirks. *The sunlight covers up the relatively dim light of the stars, but at night ... hmmm ... just like the Aurora; it's out there in the sky ... somewhere.*

He raises his hand above his head and turns his body in a slow 360 degrees, but the amount of energy it releases is essentially imperceptible by current radar or other detection methods.

He quickly changes his attitude, shaking his fist in the air and grimacing.

"From two hundred miles up," he says to no one, "we can see a picture of Snoopy on a beach towel in Maui, but we can't find a one-hundred-foot plane because it's invisible? Bullshit! They'd better find her. And soon!"

Making his way to the café, he gets himself a cup of coffee and one to go for each of the secretaries.

"Might as well play nice, could be my last cup as a free man," he says, as his words trail-off snickering bitterly.

He sits for a moment at one of the tables and enjoys a hot sip. The softness of the morning air reminds him of a simpler time — a time when the military fought for real reasons, when the sacrifice mattered; a time when family meant something, when life had meaning. Now, all the electronic crap invades the very essence of human life.

The Colonel heaves a heavy sigh.

"Well, I better get to it," he says.

He stands, turns and starts walking toward the HQ building, when both secretaries come stepping briskly around the corner. He swallows and offers a salute.

"Mr. Secretaries."

Without so much as an acknowledgement, Secretary Mallory says. "Sit."

Annoyed at the lack of respect, the Colonel narrows his eyes and grinds his teeth. Trying not draw attention, he reluctantly obeys, taking a seat across from Secretary Dow.

Secretary Dow asks, "Have you found our plane?"

"Nellis scrambled eight jets and picked up the Aurora on both airborne and ground radar stations. They tracked it for over five minutes on a westerly heading, then, a few minutes later, it turned southwest. That's when Brigadier General Dyer authorized the missile launch."

Secretary Mallory abruptly rises to his feet and says, "He did what?"

"Mr. Secretary, sir …" the Colonel sputters.

"That's my six billion dollar plane you're talking about, and you want to blow it up? What the hell were you thinking?"

The Colonel tilts his head and stares at the Secretary of Defense's face. "Mr. Secretary … With all due respect, sir, the stolen Aurora is a Mach 5+ reconnaissance fighter/bomber with advanced stealth technology. According to Nellis, after the attack it just vanished."

"So it was shot down then?"

"No, it disappeared from all radar screens. If the plane was damaged or destroyed by the missiles, the debris would have been easy to track. The consensus of Nellis is that the aircraft somehow survived."

"Have they located it then?"

"Not yet. We do have a potential lead though. About thirty minutes ago, the satellites picked up an atmospheric anomaly over the eastern Pacific Ocean, just off the Mexican coast. We don't know if it's a natural phenomenon or the Aurora, but my electronics and stealth expert is arriving shortly, and we'll review all the data."

"What expert?"

"Dr. Felix Schroder. The Aurora's stealth capabilities are a direct result of his work. If anyone can find her, he can."

"So, in the meantime, our aircraft could be anywhere in the world right now, in the hands of anyone: the Russians, the Syrians, the Koreans, the Chinese, or hell, even my grandmother, and we have no way of knowing. Is this what I'm hearing?" Dow is now shouting and visibly shaking in rage.

Clenching his teeth, the Colonel replies. "Sir, yes sir. We have our best technicians on it ..."

Secretary Dow raises his hand and says, "We've already spoken to the President, and based upon everything you've said, we must initiate operation dry dock."

"Sir?" The Colonel says with an anxious look.

Secretary Mallory leers. "Secretary Dow will oversee all operations here at Groom Lake, effective immediately. A full lockdown of all personnel will be initiated. All off-base personnel will be expected to report for duty within six hours. A full background of the past year's activities will be launched. There is a good chance that our thieves know someone working here at the base. I intend to find out whom."

Stunned, the Colonel can do nothing but look blindly at the Secretaries.

Secretary Mallory continues.

"I'm returning to Washington, where I'll begin coordinating all activities from the Pentagon. This is now considered a national security threat as it is assumed the Aurora has fallen into the wrong hands. The President has granted me temporary authority to use the CIA, the FBI, and even available Secret Service field operatives to uncover who has the plane and for what reason. The DEFCON level will be raised to 3, along with increasing the terrorist threat to orange.

"All Navy vessels and Air Force stations around the world will be put on immediate alert for any suspicious activity. NORAD will commence high resolution satellite imagery, as well as atmospheric anomaly monitoring.

"Finally, I want names of any and all living military pilots in our global database, whether active or retired. If what Nellis is telling us is true, the pilots who flew that plane must have had some special training as test pilots, instructors, or similar combat experience. We need to follow the pilot trail and fast."

The Colonel tips his coffee mug, gingerly pressing it to his lips, and takes a large swallow. The morning started out a bit hectic with the early morning meeting schedule; nothing really out of the ordinary. Now, only a few short hours later, it's as if the United States is at war.

At this point, they have to assume every country is the enemy until proven otherwise. A plan the Colonel is familiar with and unfortunately knows is doomed to failure. The severe strain on resources it creates will ultimately be their undoing. He only hopes they can catch a break and narrow the search down to what country or organization is behind the theft. At least then, they can focus their efforts.

After a few moments of discussion, the three men return to the main HQ lobby. They say their respectful goodbyes to Secretary Mallory, then Miss Berk, the base secretary, accompanies Secretary Dow to a temporary office, allowing the Colonel to return to his.

The Colonel closes the door behind him and walks to the window. *What a beautiful, picturesque morning, or at least it could have been,* he thinks. He sees the commuter 737 taxiing up to the main hanger; it slows and finally stops as the ground operator crosses his orange wands over his head. The jet engines cycle down while the stair truck starts up and slowly inches forward, toward the aircraft door.

A few seconds later, the employees and military personnel begin to walk down the ramp. Colonel Landis is ashamed to think one of these highly regarded people may be involved in one of the worst military thefts in U.S. history.

Chapter 7
The Unexpected Arrival
Over southwestern Colombia, South America

"Hold on Professor, here we go again." Doc says as they pass through Mach 1.

Her approach to the aircraft's transonic gyrations will be different this time. The Aurora abruptly rolls to the left before strongly pitching up. She continues with the left bank, rolling, completely inverted. Now, aggressively pulling back on the stick causes the beast of a plane to fall onto its back, ending in a steep dive.

"Perfect." Doc smiles. She likes the fact that she's already getting to know her new baby very well.

As a graduate of the United States Air Force Academy, with high honors, at twenty years of age, Doc is one of the very few women ever chosen to pilot F-15s and F-16s. After seven years, she became a Captain, which earned her the respect and admiration of her peers. Her unique piloting skills attracted the attention of the top brass in the Air Force, and they eventually offered her the opportunity to be a part of the SR-71 reactivation program. She flew SR-71s for four years, until another opening presented itself at Area 51, to fly for NASA, the DOD and the Air Force, collecting high speed and high altitude aerodynamic data. To say she loved to fly was the greatest understatement someone could use to describe Doc.

As she analyzes the information from the Aurora's instrumentation, Doc feels more alive than she's felt in many months. And while the controls of the most advanced aircraft in the world are at her hands, she's elated and savoring every moment.

To prevent accidental sonic booms from reaching the ground, Doc decelerated at altitude before initiating the subsonic power descent. Their orders are to perform a flyover before landing. Esteban, the leader of RAFCO, wants everyone at the camp to celebrate the arrival of the American technology.

She winces, blinks, and puts on her game face. Very soon, when they land, she'll have to resume her role as the rogue pilot who hates the U.S. enough to turn over a billion dollar piece of technology to terrorists. That thought alone is going to give her a heart attack before her time, if she lives to make it out of this shit hole of a camp.

No time like the present to tie up a loose end, she thinks.

She presses the mic button, and asks, "So are we agreed?"

"Yes, we are. I'm sure they'll completely buy it once I show them the logs," Professor says. Then he adds, chuckling, "Assuming of course, that they can read English."

"Any idea yet how we're going to get time away from the Marquez brothers?"

After signing on with PVL to do this undercover RAFCO mission, Doc and Professor worked their way into the trust of the local Colombians by hanging out in the bars and taverns near the Panamanian border.

Almost a year ago, Wolverine gathered intelligence on some unusual activity reported near Dibulla, a small town northeast of Cartagena, Colombia. The information included a report of an oil refinery under construction; but at the time, no one could find anything tying it to RAFCO. A hidden gem in the operatives' report was the location of a few seedy bars supposedly frequented by RAFCO members. Those bars became a second home to Doc and Professor as they built rapport with the locals.

Doc and Professor's undercover story was that they were ex-military test pilots forced out of service to make way for unmanned aircraft. In their words, *the Air Force eliminated them because of their fucking pay grade.* They made it a point to spew hatred and loathing of anything American during their time in those bars.

If it had taken more than a few weeks for RAFCO to hear their story and contact them, Doc was sure her liver would have failed, and she'd have made the trip home in a body bag. She was never much of a drinker, but she learned to down alcohol like the big fishes during those days, because it seemed like every time she and Professor started slamming the U.S. government and its military, someone would step up to buy a round of drinks for the U.S. bashers.

When their story finally made its way to the ears of Fernando Quintero, the RAFCO number two in command, the Reapers had almost given up hope that they were in the right area. Then, after two weeks of drinking with the locals, Doc and Professor met the Marquez brothers, sent by Fernando to check out their story.

Apparently, RAFCO was always on the lookout for pilots willing to join their cause. And as long as they passed the approval of the Marquez brothers, they would have a chance to meet Fernando for themselves.

After the Reapers had a few social chats with the brothers to boost rapport, a more serious meet-n-greet was scheduled close to the RAFCO HQ, located in the more remote southwestern area of Colombia. On the way, the brothers drugged Doc and Professor, spiking their water bottles with a mild sedative. Because Esteban Bertiz, the

RAFCO global leader, was planning to attend this meeting, Fernando was taking no chances. He ordered the Marquez brothers to bind and blindfold the Reapers as a safety measure.

When they woke up in an empty warehouse, Professor, disoriented and believing his and Doc's cover was blown, began lashing out at everyone within striking distance. He was certain their captors were planning an interrogation right before executing them.

His rational was simple: *I might as well take a few of them down in the process.*

After Professor was subdued, much to the Reapers' surprise, RAFCO was exalted by their aggressive behavior. Esteban and Fernando now believed the Reapers' story was true, that they really were rogue pilots willing to sacrifice and do anything for their beliefs. After an hour and a half of discussion, they were granted provisional membership in RAFCO, with the Marquez brothers assigned to watch them. This was a common procedure for newcomers in any group, especially one that funds terrorist activities. The fact that Doc and Professor were also fighter pilots probably added to the degree of nervousness for their new friends.

The Reapers figured their escorts would be only for a short time, leaving them alone from time to time like regular

RAFCO associates. This would give them the opportunity to begin their investigation and gather more intel to report back to PVL, as originally planned.

Unfortunately, it didn't work out that way. The Marquez brothers followed them everywhere, and the Reapers were never allowed off camp grounds. Even after months of devout service to RAFCO, Esteban was still uncertain of his new pilots' loyalty, so he decided to use them as part of his ultimate plan to get back at the United States, and the western world as a whole.

His reasoning to those who believed the loyalty of the Reapers was beyond reproach was that the rogue pilots were expendable. If the U.S. captured or killed them, no great loss; if they succeeded, they would be valued members of RAFCO and he would own their souls forever.

At first, Doc and Professor were having fun with the wingsuit training. It was an exhilarating sensation flying almost like a bird. For several weeks, whenever they asked why all the training was necessary, they got the same response: "We'll let you know when it's right." They figured it was some sort of test to prove devotion, courage, allegiance, or something like that, so they bided their time … too much time actually.

The Reapers grew frustrated with the Marquez brothers, who stuck to them like shadows, but they stopped short of asking for release from their watch. They had gathered only a tiny amount of piecemeal intel by that time, so they thought it necessary to maintain their passive stance, hoping they'd be granted full RAFCO membership soon.

Back in the cockpit of the Aurora, Doc sends the aircraft into a steep dive and presses the mic button.

"Puked yet?" Doc says.

The Aurora was dropping at a remarkable rate, enough that most city pilots would have lost their breakfast.

"That all you got?" Professor says.

"Well, if we have to give them a fly-over, we might as well do it up right. It'll only benefit our cover."

"I'm with you. Give them a show, Doc."

The RAFCO HQ, located near El Charco in southwestern Colombia, would be a beautiful tropical area for vacationing, if it wasn't the camp of a global terrorist organization.

Located in a horseshoe-shaped valley with the open end facing west toward the Pacific Ocean, steep tree-covered hills surround three-fourths of the RAFCO camp.

With the edge of the camp ridges reaching one thousand four hundred feet, only a few passages cut through the peaks, making the secluded camp difficult to traverse on foot when traveling off the cleared pathways. The main runway, with various sized outbuildings lining both sides of the mile-and-a-half concrete landing strip, separates the compound nearly in half.

Now, below five thousand feet, Doc eases back on the stick as she begins to level out the rate of descent. Professor continues to scan the area for local air traffic.

"Still a green for the all clear, Doc. Go for it. Show 'em why we're the best, Tara."

She grins, but replies in a slightly quavering voice. "Roger, Ken."

"Come on! Say it like you really mean it. We can't ever show them uncertainty. We are now committed to this mission. It's you and me to the end, Tara, no matter what."

"Roger, Ken!" she says again, with more conviction.

That's more like it, Professor thinks, smiling. As long as he can keep Doc focused on their main objective, and not the horrible thing they've done by stealing the Aurora, maybe they can successfully defeat this group of terrorists before they can do harm.

Tara and Ken are the undercover names for Doc and Professor that PVL picked for this mission. He selected the names before they left; names he thought were simple and fitting of their personalities and heritage.

At a thousand feet, Doc pushes the throttles forward and draws back on the stick hard; the g forces shove the Reapers into their seat cushions. Their facial features, now badly distorted, feel like a flattened orange.

The discomfort has no effect on Doc's concentration and precision. She masterfully watches the altimeter until the two-hundred-foot line is crossed. Leveling out, she turns east and punches the throttle.

Within seconds, the aircraft rockets over RAFCO's main runway at nearly six hundred knots. The rush of air smashes into the ground, knocking two guards off their feet and picks up rocks, flinging them over a hundred feet in every direction. The crash of broken glass echoes as the pressure wave makes its way through the camp, smashing many windows. The panes of glass that survive the rush of air rattle severely within their aged and weakened frames.

Near the center of camp, the four-story main HQ building's front doors are blown open; dirt, gravel and trash are flung onto the main lobby's floor. On the HQ's rooftop patio, the chairs, tables, umbrellas, and just about anything not permanently attached to the roof, are thrown against the eastern concrete stairway wall. A pile of twisted metal now

almost completely blocks the only doorway leading to
RAFCO's elite social gathering spot.

In the fourth floor's penthouse apartment, Esteban
turns, and for one of the few times in his life, actually smiles,
saying, "They did it."

He heads to the now empty window frame, not caring
that the glass is shattered and strewn across his room; he
barely notices the glass that crunches under his feet.
Stretching to look out the window, he gets a glimpse of the
black beast that is soon to be his. Making a fist, he pumps his
hand up and down and says, "Yes." He motions to the other
RAFCO associates currently in his room, and they head for
the runway, bounding their way down the building's four-
story stairway.

"Nicely done, Doc," Professor says.

As the Aurora passes the far end of the camp, she
initiates a vertical climb and throttles back the engines,
bleeding off most of the aircraft's speed. In an almost
hammerhead maneuver, she snap rolls the plane and starts to
descend. Aligned with the runway, she says, "It's going to be
closer than I thought. Hang on; guess it's time to test the
gear's strength."

Doc realizes the length of the runway is barely long
enough for a plane of the Aurora's impressive size to land.

Without the benefit of a drag chute or thrust reversers, the aircraft will require at least seven thousand feet of runway to stop, maybe more.

Flying at only a few miles per hour above stall, the aircraft dances toward the runway threshold. It looks more like a huge black duck tumbling out of the sky than a multi-billion dollar spy plane on final approach.

With the skill and precision that is Doc's hallmark, she places the main wheels directly onto the runway ID number, 29. Immediately, she chops the engine while keeping the nose off the ground for as long as possible. The large wedge shape of the Aurora acts nicely as an air brake.

Esteban arrives at the runway just in time to see the Aurora race by, its nose wheels still many feet off the ground. Slowly turning his head to follow the aircraft's tail, Esteban clasps his fingers together and places them around the back of his neck. He shouts, "*No!*"

The runway abruptly ends at the crest of a hill; a small hill, but very capable of stopping the aircraft if it overshoots the edge, damaging it beyond means. He is gravely concerned that his soon to be prized aircraft is about to be a pile of twisted metal.

"Doc," Professor says through the comm system.

"I got her. I could tell, while taxiing at Area 51, that she has a good braking system. I want to bleed off as much airspeed as possible so as not to risk overheating them. I'd hate to blow a tire here. We don't have any spares, you know."

Finally, she settles the nose onto the pavement and begins to brake, hard. Moments later, the screech reverberates off the surrounding buildings, hangers and woods.

The Reapers are jarred forward, snapping their seat harnesses tight against their chests and shoulders, while the unevenness of the pavement bounces them around in the cockpit. As if perfectly planned, the plane comes to rest atop the number 11. Taking a deep breath and closing her eyes just for a moment, Doc lets it out slowly, knowing the time has come to put on Tara's game face.

She flips a few switches, and the soft whine of the engines subsides.

Before turning off the electrical power, she says. "I'd like to speak on behalf of the crew and thank you for flying Reaper airlines. Please join us for our next flight to beautiful Leavenworth County, Kansas, where several new vacancies have opened up in the modest, but medium security facility that offers apartments, completely furnished, with meals included."

"Doc ... Doc ... Doc," Professor says.

He can't help but smile though, because she sounded so convincing and serious. "Have faith. You know PVL will be able to make a deal for us once we return the plane and bring RAFCO down."

"I pray you're right," Doc says. "Unfortunately, PVL has no idea what we've gotten ourselves into, but if anyone can save our butts from a lifetime in jail, it's PVL."

Chuckling and trying to relax, she adds, "We are probably number one on the most wanted list now."

The Reapers shut down the electronics and pop the canopy. The warm, humid tropical air invades their cockpit. Standing up, they turn to see numerous vehicles racing toward them.

"At least they're waving, not pointing guns at us; that's a good sign." Professor says.

Doc steps over the edge and climbs down, followed by Professor. Now, finally standing on solid ground, the magnitude of the past few hours overwhelms them. Filled with dozens of mixed emotions, they embrace and share a quiet moment before the storm of RAFCO reality hits them.

Chapter 8
It Begins
Near Port Harcourt, Nigeria

"Easy, easy," Gwami Keita says. Reaching up, he grabs one of the chains, trying to stop the over swing of the second crate. The sweat runs off his forehead in rivers, soaking everything it touches. Even at night, the Nigerian coast has minimal relief from the blistering heat. The humidity on any given day is over ninety percent, which makes strenuous or stressful work that much more uncomfortable.

After a bit of a struggle, he and his men get the forty-foot crate stabilized. Looking skyward, he waves his hand to the crane operator, directing him to continue lowering the crate into the cargo hold, placing it gently next to the one previously loaded.

The Arianna, a specially modified oil tanker, is typically used to smuggle drugs. The forward-most oil hold is split, creating a small, undocumented cargo area. The long crate barely fits in this tightly concealed location.

Already two hours behind schedule, and not wanting to draw any attention when normal operations resume in a few hours, Gwami is eager to get this thing secured.

For a moment, his mind drifts to thoughts of a cold drink and a warm woman; in other words, a better life than the one he currently has. Lately, he'd been questioning his decision to take on the additional jobs over the past year, smuggling for the RAFCO thugs. The enormous strain of the midnight loads shows in the wrinkles around his eyes and the mostly grey hair on his head, what was left of it. At age thirty-two, he looks more like an old man than one in his prime.

Pointing while raising his voice at one of the deck hands, he says. "Secure those straps to the forward latch point."

Closely supervising every aspect of the loading, he knows his life would be over if it was ever discovered that he is a smuggler.

"All set, Captain," one of the deck hands says while looking up out of the hold. Both crates are now safely secured for the trip.

"Alright then, everyone out," Gwami says. "Seal this up and get some shut eye. We leave at 0900."

He motions to the crane operator who quickly retracts the cable before shutting down the rig.

Heading for the bridge to check the last minute weather forecast, Gwami scans the various screens, looking for any unusual patterns that might impact their two-week trip to the oil refinery on the northern Colombian coast. The recently expanded facility near Dibulla is now one of the largest in Colombia. The data shows favorable weather conditions for most of the trip. He focuses on a low-pressure system currently building in the eastern Caribbean near Barbados.

We'll have to watch this one closely. These babies have the potential to develop into a tropical system, he ponders. *We might need to adjust our course the last few days between Grenada and Aruba.*

Satisfied with all the trip preparations, Gwami decides to get some shut eye. On these boats, the Captain's quarters are nothing special. Gwami has never been a complainer; he's happy with a comfortable place to collapse his tired body. A cool breeze, a stiff drink, and he's sound asleep.

A few hours later, his cell phone rings. Gwami rolls over, groans, and finally reaches, swiping the phone off the nightstand. "Ya," he snarls while looking at the clock, 05:00. *This better be good,* he thinks, wanting to smash the phone against the hull.

Reaper Two-Six
Year 6

"Yes. Yes, Mr. Bertiz. It is possible, but …" is all he's able to blurt out. While listening, he raises his hand, resting it on his temple in a look of worry. "Okay, sir."

Hanging up the phone, Gwami rolls over on the bed, coming to rest on his back. A bead of sweat slips down the side of his forehead and drips onto the pillow. He looks over at his nightstand, rubs his hand against the two-day stubble on his chin, grabs the bottle, and takes a deep swallow.

"Ah!" he says, setting the vodka back down. "RAFCO. Why did I ever get involved with these people? I thought it would be simpler to smuggle arms than drugs."

"Ya … right," he blurts to the empty cabin.

Looking at the ceiling, his eyes dance around as he wonders how he will explain this one. Fernando Quintero, RAFCO's number two, will be joining them for the voyage to Colombia. *Mr. Bertiz assured me that it was for our own benefit. When we reach our destination, it will be an advantage to have a native Colombian onboard should any custom issues develop.*

"Customs?" he mumbles in disgust. "We are a commercial tanker. At today's prices, the last thing the big refineries want is to run dry of crude oil. I think customs issues are the least of my concerns.

Reaper Two-Six
Year 6

"Getting those damn missiles, or whatever the hell they are, off my boat can't happen soon enough," he mutters.

Sitting up, he rolls to the side and pulls himself out of bed. His body still aches from last night's work, but now he is mentally wide awake.

"I might as well get my run in. An extra mile or two will do me good this morning. Hopefully, it'll calm me down before our unplanned guest arrives."

Still feeling the sluggishness of the early morning, he manages to peel off his sweat soaked clothes, dropping them in a heap next to the closet.

"That ought to keep the rats out of my room," he says. The odor offends even him.

Slipping on his crisp, clean Nike running attire, and topping off his outfit with a sleek Nigerian green headband, Gwami clicks open his cabin door. The onshore breeze greets him in the face. He takes a deep breath, and slowly closes his eyes. He then smiles and exhales, thanking the cool, welcoming air as it flows past his body.

One trip around the Arianna's upper deck is just over a quarter of a mile. *Hmmm*, he thinks. "I'd better do twenty laps this morning or I'm liable to mouth off at Fernando," he mumbles, still annoyed by this last minute bullshit. "At least

by then, I should be too tired to argue with him, just wanting
to get underway."

After almost ten minutes of stretching, Gwami jogs
down the starboard side, heading for the bow. Looking like a
firefly dancing through the night, his shirt radiates a soft
glow from the blazing deck lights.

A few miles away, in his cozy Nigerian hotel room,
Fernando is finished packing his personal affects. He has
been in Nigeria for the past three weeks, supervising the
transportation and delivery of the two crates from their
Ukrainian dealer. Walking around the room, gathering
clothes and weapons, he holds the cell phone between his
right chin and shoulder, and says, "The boat is leaving at
nine?"

"Yes," Esteban says from his RAFCO penthouse in
Colombia. "He'll add you to the manifest. The Nigerians are
sticklers about the ship's passenger list, so don't make a big
deal about it. Once out of port, we're all set on our end."

"How's our new toy?"

"Needs some sort of engine sensor repair. I'm going
to have to trust Tara and Ken. No one here has dealt with the
newer American electronics," Esteban finishes, with a bit of
hesitation.

Reaper Two-Six
Year 6

He's still not comfortable allowing their newest pilots too much responsibility or freedom for the upcoming mission.

"Hmmm," Fernando says.

"My sentiments exactly. We'll keep tabs on them twenty-four hours a day, but we need their electronics expertise for navigation, fire control, radar, and now this fucking engine issue. I don't see a way around it."

"We're still using Antonio and Ramirez, right?"

"Absolutely. They're commitment is without question, and I have confidence they can learn the electronics and other necessary items to successfully pilot the first mission."

Esteban walks over to the window and slowly slides the blinds apart. From almost a half-mile, the soft glow from the hanger housing the Aurora is still visible; it brings a smile to his face. *Soon,* he thinks … *soon …*

Fernando pops the clip out of his handgun and checks it; it's full.

Good, he thinks, smacking the clip hard into the handle. Scanning the room for any remaining items, he says, "Our second shipment is scheduled for transport to Nigeria in five weeks. Four crates this time."

Reaper Two-Six
Year 6

"Are we going to use the Arianna for the final leg again?"

"Not confirmed," Fernando grumbles, knowing full well that Esteban knows this. *What the hell?* he thinks. *Is he testing me? Me? After eighteen years, he'd better not question my loyalty.*

Annoyed by Esteban's insinuation, Fernando sits down at the tiny hotel desk and swiftly unscrews the cap on the bottle of tequila. Downing a large gulp, he continues: "It depends how this trip goes. If the Arianna's captain plays it smart, then yes, if he has room for all four. He seems very uneasy, a bit unexpected, especially for an experienced drug smuggler."

The RAFCO officers chat for an additional fifteen minutes. With smiles on both of their faces, they finish their conversation by saying, "el caos y triunfante (chaos and triumphant)."

Bidding farewell for the next two weeks, the thousand-fold retaliation plan has officially been put into action.

Chapter 9
Battle of Boyacá

"GPS, dead reckoning and inertial navigation can be used separately or combined." Professor says, pointing toward a number of switches and buttons in the cockpit.

From the Aurora's rear seat, Ramirez Alvarez continues to sort through various screens and menu options of the integrated navigation, fire control and radar systems. After a few minutes of discussion, Ramirez looks up and acknowledges, seeming to finally understand Professor's instructions.

Originally from Bulgaria, Ramirez flew MiG-29s for nearly fifteen years before joining RAFCO. A well-sculpted, muscular man of just over six feet, he complements his physique with an impressive understanding of avionics and aeronautics. Professor was hoping to limit the amount of knowledge they would be expected to provide RAFCO, but Ramirez's tenacity and intellect is making that almost impossible.

For the past ten days, Professor has been teaching Ramirez the aircraft's back seat operations, while Doc has been focusing on pilot functions with RAFCO's chief pilot,

Antonio Mendez. Antonio is an experienced Su-35 pilot for the Venezuelan Air Force, and the complete opposite of Ramirez. Standing only five feet, four inches, and weighing almost one hundred, eighty pounds, Antonio does not look like the ideal military pilot. He is short, pudgy, and looks soft; however, in the front seat, his razor focus and amazingly smooth and efficient motor skills shine. He also has an insatiable desire to know everything about the aircraft's capabilities. Doc was told he studies her prepared notes far into the night, coming to class with a new list of questions the next day.

Under normal circumstances, she would love her student's intensity, but providing intimate details of the Aurora's design and specifications to a RAFCO pilot is beginning to make her nauseous. Every time she closes her eyes, she sees the courtroom of her trial in her mind. She can also hear the judge's sentence, "You are hereby found guilty of treason, and this court sentences you to life in prison. Guards, take her away to her new cell in Leavenworth." The imaginary smack of the judge's gavel sends shivers down her spine.

The fourteen hours-a-day marathon training sessions have left both Doc and Professor looking almost ill. Their facial features are drawn, and their eyes are bloodshot. Even

Doc's voice has become raspy. She thought it was maybe a new allergy to mold, or something in the jungle environment exasperating her airways, but now she knows it's because she's had to talk for hours on end to her "student."

This was not the plan, Professor thinks during a short, quiet moment away from Ramirez's constant badgering. *We were going to keep the Aurora's secrets to ourselves, showing them only how to operate it on a basic level. It would be no different than sharing information you can find on the Internet about a typical fourth generation military fighter.*

"Fuck," Professor blurts, unexpectedly. He meant for that to be kept quiet.

"Whaaaaat?" Ramirez responds, quickly turning to face Professor.

"Oh, sorry," Professor says tugging at his shirt-tail, "I snagged my dang shirt on the sharp edge of this canopy railing." He fakes a frown and then shrugs, saying, "It's my favorite shirt."

Hoping to distract Ramirez, Professor continues to point and explain the function of the various instruments, buttons and switches in front of him. *Blind them with bullshit,* he thinks, desperately trying not to crack a smile ... *and maybe we can still outwit them.*

Reaper Two-Six
Year 6

As the day ends, the Marquez brothers escort the Reapers to their suite, at least that's what RAFCO calls their meager quarters. The room consists of two beds separated by a sheet for privacy, a vanity with a cracked mirror and cold running water, a few small clothing storage bins, a stand-up shower and a two-person table and chairs. By conservative estimates, the suite is anything but comfortable.

Essentially, the Reapers are under house arrest. Their daily whereabouts are continuously monitored by the Marquez brothers. Then, after the evening meal, the brothers lock them in their suite until the following morning.

"Goodnight," Doc says to Carlos Marquez. He nods and firmly closes the door. Immediately she hears the sound of the deadbolt slide home, quickly followed by the latching of the chain. They are once again locked in for the night.

"You'd think we were criminals," Doc says quietly to Professor when she hears the brothers walking down the hallway, loudly talking about something in Spanish.

"To them, we are, Doc. All they know is that we are willing to go along with their plans because we hate the U.S. They don't know anything else about us. Like whether or not we regret our decision and will bolt the first opportunity we get. You can't really blame them for that." Then he adds, in a low voice, "If they only knew …"

"We'd be dead by now," Doc says, not wanting to go where Professor was leading. She has those nightmares all on her own, and doesn't need to bring them to light.

Doc shakes her head in disgust and heads to the bathroom to begin her nightly routine. She showers first, while Professor listens to the hallway noises and taking note of any activity outside. Their window faces south, looking over the main runway, directly across from the main HQ building. After about thirty minutes, they reverse roles. Then, before the night is over, they compare notes and make a summary timeline with names, events, places, and observations.

Within the first few days upon entering the camp, the Reapers made a small incision into the wooden flooring in the bathroom, behind the toilet. Using pressure and moisture, they were finally able to pry it up, creating a small trap-door in the flooring. This is where they've hidden their logs and notes since arriving at RAFCO, over six months ago.

Doc looks at her watch, 22:10, and nods to Professor. He turns out the room lights and carefully stashes the evening's notes away, setting the flooring back into place. Normally, the Reapers would attempt to get some rest before their 0700 wake-up call, but tonight is different.

The Battle of Boyacá celebration is tonight; a yearly August 7 holiday. This Colombian festival commemorates the battle when Colombia acquired its independence from Spain.

Esteban has great respect for the spirit and strength of the men who fought for his country's independence two hundred years ago. In many ways, RAFCO aims to be like the armies of that era. So, every year, he arranges for an off-camp celebration for all his officers and associates. It has become almost a right-of-passage event for all the previous years' new associates. All full membership associates are eligible for a promotion to second lieutenant after one year of service. A highlight of the Battle of Boyacá RAFCO celebration is the announcement of this year's officer promotions.

When Professor signals to Doc that the last of the vehicles has left the camp, she carefully removes the glass from their window. Over the last week, the Reapers slowly chipped away the spackling holding the glass in the frame. When they arrived at the camp with the Aurora, Doc's flyby stunt had given them an unexpected side benefit — the windows in many areas of the camp had been smashed or shaken loose from their frail mountings, and no replacements had yet been installed. They decided to use this fact to their advantage.

Slipping out the window of their first story suite, both Doc and Professor take refuge in a nearby garage. Scanning the vast expanse of the runway in front of them, they prepare themselves. Rather than wasting more than thirty minutes each way to circle around the runway in the shadows, they make the bold decision to dash across the wide-open runway, a minute or so apart, then meet back at their suite in forty-five minutes.

Professor darts across the runway, sneaks inside the hanger next to the main HQ building, and begins looking for anything that will help the Reapers determine what RAFCO is planning.

Doc takes off and successfully traverses the pavement, quickly circling to the back of a storage building directly opposite the garage. Looking up, toward the main HQ building on her right, she smiles, seeing that it was true; Esteban's windows are smashed and still wide open.

Looking like a scene from an Uncharted series video game, with cat-like swiftness and deft movements, Doc scales the side of the building, clawing her way from window to porch ledge, then to window, to drain pipe, and finally, to the sill of Esteban's penthouse. Slowly, she peeks inside.

Seeing nothing but blackness, she pulls herself inside the room.

She rests for a few seconds, breathing through the aches in her shoulder muscles that twitch from the strain of the climb. She has been unable to maintain her weight lifting routine for the past several months while undercover, not wanting to attract unwanted attention.

Reaching down, she clicks her watch. A warm, bright glow emanates from around the face as tiny LED lights come to life.

"Now, let's find out what the fuck is going on around here," She says, softly.

After Doc hunts through as much of the penthouse as their agreed upon time allows, she climbs out the window and down the four-story structure. She catches a glimpse of Professor climbing into their suite's window before she sprints across the runway.

Now, safely back inside their suite, she approaches Professor.

She reaches over, taps him on the back and then hands him an iPhone 4S. Stunned, he carefully takes it. As if holding a newborn infant, he cradles it in his hand, staring at it intensely. He turns to look at Doc, then back at the phone.

In a sudden panic, he remembers that RAFCO has extensive electronics monitoring in the camp. They are sure to have high ranking RAFCO associates iPhone's listed as a top priority on that monitoring list. He voices his concern to Doc. "This may not have been such a good idea, Doc. What if ..."

Doc hears a sound in the hallway and motions to Professor with her finger over her lips.

When the Reapers discovered the extensive camp-wide electronic monitoring system, they decided to cover up their imbedded GPS beacons with a metallically infused temporary tattoo to insure that no accidental transmissions occurred. For search and recovery purposes, all Reapers had a homing beacon sewn into their flight suit that activates when excessive G loads occur, during a crash or an ejection.

Reaper command can also activate the beacon remotely, if needed. The remote activation uses an encrypted satellite message, but the beacon's transmission could be easily picked up by standard monitoring systems. With proper technique, an enemy could, in theory, locate the source of the transmission very accurately.

For the covert RAFCO mission, Doc and Professor were fitted with a newer generation beacon, placed surgically under their skin. The procedure began with a small incision on the outer part of the upper arm, near the shoulder; then the device was carefully implanted deep into the muscle tissue. The excessive g loads and remote activation are standard, but the new device came with an additional feature, allowing for automatic activation when the sensor detects abnormally low temperatures, typically indicating the death of the pilot. Once synced with the body's normal temperature profile, the device automatically begins transmitting its location when exposed to temperatures less than sixty degrees Fahrenheit (sixteen degrees Centigrade).

Doc rolls her eyes at Professor, and says, "Don't you think I knew that before I took the iPhone from the apartment? Anyway, for some reason the external antenna is disabled. Right now, it isn't sending or receiving shit. My guess is that's why one of Esteban's cronies accidently left it behind before heading for the celebration. And before you ask, I have no idea why they'd have a cell phone that doesn't work as a cell phone off camp. You'd have to crawl into Crazy Town to figure that one out," she adds.

After a long pause, she continues, "I noticed a unique Wi-Fi frequency, and I guess that's how they keep track of everyone, as well as some sort of camp-wide communication system. I hacked into the settings and turned it off. Hopefully, that'll keep it from being discovered. They might even think the phone has been accidently damaged or destroyed."

She shakes her head in frustration and a bit of outrage that Professor thought she wouldn't fully check out the phone before bringing it back to the suite. After taking a few moments to simmer down, she decides to just forget about it. *We're both on edge,* she thinks, *and the extra paranoia is probably a good thing; checking each other's back.*

Gently, Professor pushes the power button and watches as the screen comes to life. The photo app is already active and open. He flips through some of the images, taking mental notes of various photos that he needs to review in more detail. After a few minutes, he looks over at Doc and smiles, as if to say, *"You sneaky little bitch."*

She returns the smile and reaches out her hand, "I have one in particular I want you to see."

She quickly shuffles through the various images, finally locating one of special interest. Handing the phone back to Professor, she waits to see his expression.

After minutes of intense study, he swallows hard, rolls his head in her direction, and shakes it back and forth.

"Exactly," she says, her tone soft and affirming.

"They're planning to invade the U.S., Europe and Australia at the same time? Are you serious? There is no fucking way RAFCO can invade them all at once. They don't have the resources."

Doc nods in agreement and lets Professor continue.

"Let's think about this. Even if they have nukes, or whatever missiles they plan to hookup to the Aurora, they might get in a first strike and take out a major city, maybe even Washington, but once the word gets out who launched it, this camp and all other RAFCO facilities around the world will be leveled by the U.S. and other NATO+ allies. Hell, maybe even by the Colombian armed forces, because they sure as hell don't want anything to do with RAFCO's shit storm. This can't be right. It has to be some twisted dream. Esteban's ideal RAFCO takes over the world dream, or his power-hungry delusions, or something. Jesus Christ!" Professor says.

When the rambling stops, Doc sits on the edge of her bunk and cradles her head in her hands. The enormity of the situation is starting to hit her like a ton of bricks; but she has to keep it together. She *must* keep it together until they devise a plan to stop RAFCO.

She feels Professor nudge her shoulder as he hands the phone back to her. Then he lies on his bunk and rolls onto his back. For about the next fifteen minutes, they are both quiet, lost in their own thoughts about the hell they helped set into motion.

Doc begins carefully flipping through the images she snapped in Esteban's suite. At the time, she didn't care to know *what* she was snapping pictures of, she was just trying to gather as much information as she could and get out. Now, as she flips through the thumbnails, she is able to begin digesting the content of the images.

Suddenly, in the photos of Esteban's email messages, she sees something that causes her to freeze. There, at the bottom of the image is a name: Choe Dong-Ju.

It can't be, she thinks. *Choe Dong-Ju?*

Her eyes drift from the iPhone's screen, now wandering around the room as her mind races. A minute later, the phone goes blank as the automatic power saver takes hold.

A few more minutes pass before Professor notices the room is dark. Rolling once more to face her, he can see the shadow of her outlined face, the crinkles on her forehead catching his attention.

"What?" he asks.

She flips the phone to him through the air. Caught completely off guard, his heart rate soars. As if in slow motion, all he can do is watch as the phone bounces off his partially open hands, then falls onto his crotch, coming to rest against his right thigh.

Giving her a perplexed look, Professor looks back down at the phone. Seemingly unaffected by his reaction, Doc continues to look at him in some sort of daze. Professor tilts his head, narrowing his eyes in anger to have the phone hit him without an apology; but his anger subsides when he gets no reaction. He figures whatever she saw on the phone must be shocking for her to ignore common courtesy, and to be so lost in thought.

After skimming through the photographed document still on the screen, he thinks, *Choe Dong-Ju! Isn't he the leader of the North Korean National Defense Commission? Ummm, Chairman. Yeah, basically their military supreme commander, like our Secretary of Defense.*

Rolling his thumb from top to bottom on the iPhone's screen, he starts reading the document from the beginning again, this time in detail. Every so often he slides his right thumb up along the screen, scrolling the image and even zooming in from time to time.

As the end of the document nears, he utters, "Jesus."

Doc finally snaps out of her daze, purses her lips in concern, and nods in his direction. Nothing more needs explaining. The email is clear and they both now know where

RAFCO is planning to get the extra military firepower —
North Korea.

To save the battery power, Professor turns off the
iPhone. He gets up and heads to the bathroom, pretending to
use the toilet. While it flushes, he pops open the trap-door,
places the iPhone inside, and closes the flooring over it.

After leaving the bathroom, he looks over at Doc; she
is laying with her back to him, seemingly asleep. He waits
for several moments, before he settles into his own bunk. He
lies awake for hours, pondering the obvious hurdles he and
Doc must overcome.

One thing is certain, if this mission goes sour,
Professor knows he has lived his life for the GDO and the
military, never having had a wife or family of his own. For
just a moment, he feels sorry for himself, for a life he may
never live, or have the opportunity to live. However, it is a
fleeting thought that he pushes to the back of his mind as
quick as it came, thanks to his steely determination. Once he
sets his mind on something, Professor is razor-focused.

He rolls over in his bunk for about the fifteenth time
as a new thought plays at the edge of his consciousness, a
plan for what he and Doc must do next.

Doc is sleepless as well. She thinks about the new
intel, and that they have got to get it to PVL at any cost. She

knows that the RAFCO associates are not idiots, and they will catch on eventually to their true intentions.

As the night hours tick away, both Reaper's devise a plan to get the intel to PVL before their cover is blown or their room is searched.

Chapter 10
The Awakening

The next morning, Pancho Mendez, RAFCO's head aircraft mechanic, busts open the mess hall door. He stands in the open doorway for several seconds as his eyes scan the room. Finally, he locates his prey, and loudly stomps his way over to the far corner, where Professor, Doc, Antonio, Ramirez, and the Marquez brothers are having breakfast.

Smacking Professor on the shoulder, he demands in broken English, "Today you are with me. I finally got stupid temperature sensor for aircraft pre-heater. We will install today, together."

Scowling, Professor acknowledges him with a sneer and a rhetorical hand gesture. Chuckling, even RAFCO's pilots enjoy Professor's kiss-off statement.

Continuing the insult, Professor says to Pancho, "Hey, you're last name is Mendez, right?"

Pancho shrugs, wondering why this arrogant piece of shit American wants to know. "Yes, why?"

"I was just wondering if you are Antonio Mendez's brother."

That was enough to stop Pancho in his tracks. He glares at each person sitting at the table, then looks at Professor with seething hatred, and spits on the floor, missing Professor's shoes by an inch or two. "I am no related to that fucking Venezuelan pig!" he growls, pointing at Antonio.

Stomping his way back toward the door, he stops short, turns, shakes his finger at Professor and says, "Ten minutes, or your ass is history." He powers through the small dining room door, slamming it shut behind him.

The four RAFCO officers erupt in laughter, mocking Pancho's mannerisms. Ramirez shakes his finger at Professor and says, "Ten minutes ... ten minutes!"

As the officers' laugh uncontrollably, the Reapers sit in stunned silence at the disdainful attitude the RAFCO members have for each other, and especially their head mechanic.

They would never have such an adversarial relationship with their head aircraft mechanic, because his skill is literally what keeps them all alive. If Pancho had half a notion to exact revenge, Antonio and all the other RAFCO pilots wouldn't live to laugh at him ever again.

Doc and Professor look at each other, and although neither one speaks, they both know what the other is thinking. That none of the Reapers would ever disrespect another member of their team, regardless of their rank or pay grade, or job responsibility. Hell, even the janitors at the Reaper bases received more respect.

Professor didn't appreciate Pancho's abrasive demands, but he appreciated his dedication to his job, and his attention to detail while he worked on the Aurora.

Hell, it wouldn't surprise me if Pancho pulled the fuel system pump breaker just to piss off Antonio and Ramirez when they start this upcoming mission, Professor thinks. *Geesh ... What a difference between cultures and organizations.*

Professor decides it's best to quickly finish up his meal and get over to the hanger. After last night's discovery, they need to get as much time with RAFCO members as possible, trying to figure out a way to sneak a message to PVL. He stands and snaps at the brothers to hurry up; he doesn't want to piss off Pancho any more than he already has. To Professor's surprise, Carlos Marquez tells him to go on without them.

"We will catch-up with you later, after the repairs are finished."

Astonished, Professor just stands there, unsure what to do.

Waving his hand in a shooing motion, Miguel Marquez interjects, and says, "Get the fuck out of here. I will finish my coffee and not be rushed by impatient mechanics."

Antonio adds, "Those thirty seconds he was here is about all we can handle of Pancho. None of us can stand being around him more than that. He is, well, exasperating." He chuckles, before continuing, "You will see. Go now. Fix the plane and leave us to our meal."

After tossing his garbage away, Professor exits the mess hall and decides to take a quick detour to the room he shares with Doc. Moving as fast as he can without creating too much noise, he snatches the iPhone from the hiding spot and tucks it into his boot. A few minutes later, he arrives at the hanger to see a snarling Pancho.

"Fucking American technology," Pancho bellows. "Even goddamn maintenance hatches take fucking PhD to open."

Trying not to laugh or insult Pancho's intelligence, Professor offers to assist. Because of the extreme temperatures and pressures exerted on the Aurora's outer skin, the maintenance hatches required a special sealing system. A typical military style snap-opening or screw-type mechanism would never survive. Instead, the engineers designed a system of interlocking spring-loaded pins that can be accessed only from inside the aircraft. This avoids the significant issues associated with any sort of external bolting scheme, and assures tight sealing of all surfaces. The concept is similar to the locking system found on the Space Shuttle's cargo bay doors.

After opening the Aurora's canopy, Professor climbs the fuselage footholds. Bending way over, he finally locates the purple handle on the left side, near the back seat, tucked under the side panel. He pulls on it, hard.

Looking like bomber bay doors, the engine maintenance hatches fall open gently. Pancho turns away in disgust, swiping the replacement sensor from the parts rack.

"Okay. Number two is left or right side?" Pancho asks.

"Starboard," Professor replies, a little surprised. As the head mechanic, Pancho should have known that. When Pancho glares at him, Professor adds, "I mean, right."

"There," Pancho says, pointing over to the desk next to his laptop. "Sit. I will replace sensor first. Then we check to make sure it works. After, we must program computer for first mission."

Professor grudgingly complies. He sees Pancho grab several tools and disappear under the aircraft. Professor's eyes drift to the laptop; his mind begins to race with all sorts of crazy ideas. He glances over at the mechanic, still within the bay doors, and looks back at the laptop. He stretches his neck around to look at everything on the top of the desk; a moment later, quietly, he opens a few of the drawers.

Ah, yes, he congratulates himself — he's found the iPhone docking cable. He quickly grabs the cable out of the top drawer.

Looking back at the aircraft one more time, he decides to go for it. Swiftly, he pulls out the iPhone from his boot, snaps in the docking cable and plugs the other end into the laptop. A few seconds later, the file manager opens to show the available C and E drives. He creates a folder on the main computer's C-drive, buried deep within an obscure system folder tree. He names it something commonly found in system directories, hoping this will prevent the file from accidental discovery.

Quickly, he selects all the images that Doc took and copies them to the new C-drive folder. The Windows copy dialog box opens showing, 78 items and 109 Mb.

"Shit!" he mutters softly.

He glances around to see if Pancho heard him, then sighs with relief. He looks back at the screen and urges under his breath, "Come on, hurry."

The upload counter reads: twenty-five percent complete.

Reaper Two-Six
Year 6

Then: thirty-five percent complete.

Professor feels like he's going to have a panic attack, as the folder copy animation seems to go on forever.

The counter reads: fifty-five percent complete.

Good Lord, Professor groans.

He feels beads of sweat trickling down the back of his neck. He can also feel his left hand trembling ever so slightly.

Get it together, he tells himself. *You're better than this.*

Of course, the lack of sleep over the past eleven days has left him vulnerable and more sensitive to anxiety.

Come on shake it off, almost there.

The counter reads: ninety-nine percent complete.

As a drip of sweat falls from his left eyebrow, the copying process finally completes.

Thank God, he thinks.

He quickly unplugs the iPhone cable from both devices and slips it back into the desk, then closes the Windows file manager and stashes the iPhone back into his boot. Grabbing a bandana out of his pocket, he wipes his forehead and neck clean of sweat, although the heat in the midday sun and the relentless humidity are an easy explanation for sweat at any hour.

Reaper Two-Six
Year 6

Leaning back in the chair, he starts to plan his next step when Pancho yells, "Hey, lazy American! Get your ass over here. I need you to read voltmeter. You have to be goddamn octopus to work on this fucking plane. Shit!"

Professor cracks a grin. After hearing Pancho's constant griping, he can see what the RAFCO officers mean about his attitude.

I bet I can use that to my advantage somehow, he thinks. He knows he has to formulate a plan for what to do with the recently transferred images.

Over the next three hours, both Pancho and Professor have their fair share of frustrations; circuit breakers that were left open, pinched fingers while trying to tighten bolts in confined places, shorted wires, improper screw threads, and even ground power units that were not charged properly from their last usage.

By the time the engine fuel pre-heater system is fully functional, Professor shakes his head and thinks, *I bet I've heard more swear words today than I have in the past twenty days combined.*

After a fifteen-minute break for lunch, they delve into mission planning. To the Professor's surprise, Pancho knows a lot about programming the navigational system with the software on his laptop.

For the next two hours, he quietly watches Pancho enter waypoints and altitudes of the primary flight path, as well as alternatives along the planned route. In addition, he enters emergency landing sites friendly to RAFCO. Next, he turns to fire control and programming the on-board computer with the intended flight path of the missiles.

Pancho turns to Professor and asks, "Two. Yes?"

"What?"

"The plane can launch two missiles at same time?"

"Oh. Yes." Professor says, immediately wishing he had lied. The question caught him off-guard and his reply was made instinctually. For the next twenty-five minutes, he stares at the computer screen in deep thought, while Pancho enters the missile's data.

158,400 feet? Professor muses. *What in the world is going on? Why have missiles at that altitude? How the hell are you going to get it up that high?*

Pancho continues to enter the planned flight path, including speed and possible course correction time points, when another peculiar piece of data catches Professor's attention.

Fourteen hundred knots? He again mulls over this information. *For a long range air-launched missile?* He blinks at the screen, surely he's read the data wrong; but he hadn't. *That just isn't right, is it?*

Carefully trying to memorize a few select data points before Pancho finishes, Professor politely interrupts and questions him about specific pieces of information. He is stalling, so he can get more time to look at the data. After a few minutes of back-and-forth questions and answers, he senses Pancho's growing annoyance. He backs off and returns to his passive role.

His eyes continue to roam over the details, taking in everything he can, while his mind tries to make sense of the data.

For sure, something much more than what we initially expected is going on here, Professor tells himself. The desperation to get the word out to PVL grows.

Upon finishing the programming, Pancho closes the laptop, opens his desk, and pulls out an aircraft data transfer cable.

"Come on, let's finish this," he says. "You can upload it into aircraft computer."

After Professor plops down into the Aurora's rear seat, Pancho hands him the laptop and cable. He inserts the USB connector into the laptop and the other end into the aircraft's data port. Just like Doc did many days ago, he activates an

FTP program and presses Enter. The mission critical data streams through the cable and into the Aurora's brain.

Suddenly, Professor realizes just what RAFCO might be planning with this mission.

Oooohhhhh, shit, he thinks.

With the navigational data fresh on his mind, Professor swallows hard, now knowing the Reapers must stop this mission from ever happening, no matter the cost.

Chapter 11
The Transformation

Since the Aurora is not available for the day, Doc, Antonio and Ramirez enjoy an afternoon on the HQ's rooftop patio. Located directly above Esteban's penthouse apartment, it is usually reserved for high-level social gatherings and is off-limits to other personnel. Esteban's unexpected offer for them to use the patio was a complete surprise.

Doc remembered Esteban's words to his pilots that morning: "What is mine is now yours, so come, enjoy. In four days, the future of the RAFCO name will forever be known."

The three spent the day reviewing abort scenarios, navigational and engine restart procedures, fire control, threat monitoring, and a host of other topics. With Esteban's windows still broken, Doc is in a good position to do some eavesdropping between conversations.

That evening, Doc enjoys a friendly chat with other RAFCO officers in the mess hall. *Keep the happy face ... keep the happy face,* she keeps repeating. Doc must pretend she is as happy as RAFCO to see the day that America will pay. The U.S. disgraced them, and RAFCO is helping them exact their revenge. For Doc, at least, this is the most difficult role to play. She may not have always agreed with U.S. policies, but she was loyal to the cause to fight terrorists for the greater good. And here she sits among the very organization of people she loathes, drinking and smiling with them as if she belonged. Instead of smiling, she wanted to take the closest sharp object and bury it into the heart of every monster in this camp.

Pasting a smile on her face, she continues to pick out key pieces of information from the banter of the conversations close by. She puts these tidbits together with the other information she's overhead from Esteban's room earlier in the day, when she was on the patio.

Mulling it over, she completely misses Professor walking up to join them, taking the seat at the end of the long table. Once out of her daze, she notices his demeanor; extremely serious and almost ghostly, completely lost in thought.

And I thought I was having a good time, she thinks.

Fearing that someone will notice her watching Professor, Doc turns away and decides to follow the flow of the conversations, just as she's been doing for the past several months. She's dying to know what Professor is thinking about, knowing it must be something he uncovered or that happened today as he worked on the Aurora with Pancho; but catching up will have to wait.

After almost five minutes, Professor finally snaps out of his trance-like state and joins the conversation at his end of the table. He eyes Doc, even winking a few times, while engaging in the social etiquette they've endured over the many months of their undercover mission.

As he watches Doc, in an animated conversation with the Marquez brothers, Professor shakes his head in amazement.

She deserves an academy award. She is playing her role splendidly. No one has a clue she's actually extracting as much information about the camp's daily activities as possible.

Later that night, in what has become their custom; the Marquez brothers accompany the Reapers to their suite and lock them in for the night. Knowing the guard can hear their conversations through the door, they decide to adhere to their nightly routine as close as possible.

More than two hours pass before they decide it's safe to chat in low whispers. Professor begins by telling Doc about the aircraft repairs and how he sneaked the photos she took in Esteban's penthouse onto Pancho's computer. He is proud of his actions and the possibility of using it to their

advantage somehow; but that excitement is short-lived. The
anger on Doc's face is apparent.

"You did what?" Doc grinds each word out from
between her clenched teeth. She almost yells at him until she
remembers they can be overheard. She scowls at him; disgust
and horror radiates from her face. She heads over to the bed
and lies down, smacking her forehead with the palm of her
left hand. "You've sealed our fate. For sure, we're going to
be exposed and killed now. What the hell were you
thinking?"

Caught completely off-guard by her reaction, he takes
a seat on the bed next to her. Placing his hand on her
shoulder, he says softly, "Doc. I'll admit it was an impulsive
decision, with no real thought-out plan. I don't yet have an
idea how I'm going to get access to the data again, or even
what I might be able to do with it. But after the navigational
data I saw today, I'm glad that I took the chance to transfer
the image files. It's time for us to start risking everything, no
matter the consequences."

She slowly raises her eyes, locking them intensely on
his face, and begins to explain the pieces of conversations
she heard today. Professor listens carefully, absorbing every
word. After about fifteen minutes, his gaze wanders off into

the distance, continuing to evolve the picture in his head of what RAFCO is planning.

He snaps back when he hears Doc say something of concern.

"Four days?" he blurts. "Oh, shit!"

Professor looks around him, cautious, because he'd spoken too loudly. Doc rolls her eyes at him, and he acknowledges her with a frown.

"Sorry," he whispers. "We've really got to step it up then, because of what I think they are planning."

Sliding a little closer to her so they can talk quietly, he continues. "From your images, we know they are thinking about an invasion plan for the U.S., Europe and Australia; maybe even more countries are on their list that we haven't discovered yet. We both agreed it was ludicrous, even with help from North Korea; it just didn't make sense. It seems like a suicide plan to bomb away, knowing full well that eventually the combined forces of the U.S. and European military will retaliate. How can they possibly succeed?

"From what I saw in the mission data, I think they're planning to destroy the country's infrastructure. Once they succeed, a few weeks or at most a few months later, they'll just waltz right in and take over, imprisoning or killing those not willing to submit."

Doc sees the dread in his eyes. Reaching out, she gently grasps his arm, and says, "You're thinking an EMP strike aren't you?"

Professor nods.

An Electromagnetic Pulse (EMP) occurs when a nuclear device detonates at high altitude, typically above 150,000 feet. A powerful EMP attack can create unimaginable devastation; most communications will fail, and transportation systems will come to a halt, including all vehicles manufactured after 1980, with many older models vulnerable, too. The electrical power grid will be completely destroyed in the directly affected areas, contributing to a functional collapse of grids beyond the exposed areas, as the chain reaction propagates from region to region in a giant ripple effect. Due to a severe lack of replacement electrical power infrastructure components, the very fabric of today's modern society will effectively be obliterated for years. The technology on which most of the world thrives will cease to exist in any EMP affected zone.

"Are you sure?" she says, hopeful that he misunderstood what he saw.

She places her hand over her mouth and looks up at him with fear in her eyes. *How can one terrorist group hold that much power over an entire nation?* she wonders. *It can't be ... it just can't.*

Professor stands up and tiptoes over to the table, where he sits in one of the chairs. He motions for her to join him. He lights a candle, and then grabs a pen and a pad of paper. He proceeds to draw an outline of the United States.

Doc laughs at the crude drawing and says, "Good thing you're an excellent pilot, because you'd have never made it as an artist."

Professor ignores her mocking comment and continues adding dots on the crude map, each one showing the approximate location of major cities: Washington D.C., Boston, New York, Detroit, Atlanta, Dallas, St. Louis, Denver, Seattle, San Francisco, Los Angeles and Phoenix.

He draws a line, starting off the east coast of Florida. Then, continuing northward with a slight bend to the west, ending somewhere around western North Carolina. Finally, the line makes a U-turn and heads south, until it passes west of Florida.

He points to the map and says, "I believe this is the intended flight path of the Aurora's first mission."

Doc studies the map with the premise of an EMP strike, roughly calculating distances between a few cities from the supposed turnaround point. *Hmmm,* she thinks.

"Do you believe they're planning to release the missiles here?" she asks, pointing to the U-turn place on the map, "or fire them earlier and this just happens to be the point where the turn takes place?"

"Good question." Professor replies. "That brings up the second part of the information I found out today."

Doc's stunned look says it all. *And I thought I had a productive information gathering day. Sheesh. He outdid me.*

"Get this," Professor says. "The missiles' planned cruise altitude is one-hundred, fifty-eight thousand, four hundred feet; exactly thirty miles. That can't be a coincidence; it's too specific. Oh, and the planned speed of the missile is fourteen hundred knots — over Mach 2.5 at that altitude.

"A supersonic cruise missile?" she asks.

"That's my guess."

"I assume you think they're nukes?"

Professor nods, and with a strong conviction says, "Why else would you want to set a blast off at that altitude? You're not going to kill anyone, so it must be an EMP strike."

Both Reapers sit back and slump in their seats. The physical and emotional exhaustion has been overwhelming since they left Area 51 with the Aurora. They'd never have agreed to stealing it if they had any clue RAFCO was planning something this immense and destructive. The events set off by an EMP strike would have a domino effect all over the world for years, maybe decades.

As if their discussion couldn't get any worse, Professor says, "Pancho asked if the Aurora could launch two missiles simultaneously and I stupidly said yes."

Locking her eyes with his, Doc says, her tone disgusted, "Professor ..."

"I know, I know. I was lost in thought trying to memorize the flight path data when he sprang the question on me. It just came out before I realized what I was saying. Trust me, I've been kicking myself in the ass ever since."

As if in response to the mounting concern and fear of what might happen, Professor feels every muscle in his body tense, and then droop with fatigue. Even his jaw clenches, unknowingly grinding his teeth.

Trying to get more comfortable, he stands up and flips his seat around. He sits back down and rests his hands on the back of the chair.

Quietly, he says, "If you think about it, RAFCO's plan is brilliant, in a sadistic way. The Aurora can be used to fly totally undetected anywhere in the world. Once it's within a few hundred miles of the intended target, they can launch a supersonic cruise missile, most likely rocket-powered in order to fly at that high an altitude. The flight time of the missile can't be more than ten or fifteen minutes, so there is minimal radar warning. By then, good luck to the intended target country trying to shoot down a Mach 2+ missile 150,000 feet in the sky. It's highly unlikely, if not completely impossible. They can keep flying mission-after-mission until they run out of nukes.

"I believe their first two missiles are intended for the northeastern U.S., D.C. or New York, probably, and then somewhere more in the central U.S., like St. Louis. So, depending upon the size of the nuke, the entire eastern half of the country will be affected by a massive EMP strike, even reaching as far west as Colorado or Nevada."

The emotional burden of the discussion starts to drag Doc down. The enormous guilt from putting the Aurora into RAFCO's hands is starting to tear at the very core of her being. *This is my fault,* she keeps repeating in her mind. *I gave them the Aurora. I made it possible for them to rain destruction down on innocent civilians.*

As if Professor has read her mind, he tries to calm her saying, "You know this is not your fault. Yes, we provided them with the Aurora, but that in itself does not make you responsible for what they plan to do with it. The Aurora is just an instrument. RAFCO is responsible for the destruction it could do."

Doc blinks her eyes, raises her head, and tries to look thankful for Professor's words of encouragement, but she can't. The burden she now carries is just too great.

"I just wish I knew where they got the nukes they're planning to use," Professor adds. "They must have bought them from some black market dealer who is only out for a buck, not caring that he just enabled a terrorist group to wipe out an entire city's existence. The Aurora is just one of many possible delivery systems; that's it. If they didn't have the Aurora, then I'm certain they'd look to use their Chinese J-20 stealth aircraft, or their Chinese bomber, or hell, even a ground launched satellite rocket system tipped with nukes would probably do the trick."

Professor empathizes with Doc's anguish, but at the same time, he knows they need to maintain their focus and dedication, now more than ever. From Doc's information, something significant is going to happen in the next four days; he suspects either the start or completion of the first mission.

A few moments later, he looks Doc square in the eyes and says, "We must stop this mission and destroy RAFCO — *now* — no matter the cost."

Chapter 12
Revived
Arlington, Virginia, United States

"Yes, Mr. President," Secretary Mallory says. He cringes at the thought of what the President has instructed him to do. "Sir, if I can just have a few more days. We're —"

President Mason's voice cuts him off. He listens intently for the next few minutes to the President's demands, stirring his coffee aggressively, watching, unconcerned, as a couple of drops slosh over the sides of the mug onto the polished mahogany desk.

He tries not to communicate his exasperation through the phone, as he downs a large mouthful of the steamy brew. After the warm coffee soothes his nerves, he says, "Yes sir, I know it's been twelve days sir. All available global resources in the field have been diverted to recovering the Aurora.

"I just spoke with Secretary Dow at the base less than an hour ago, and he assures me they're closing in."

That was a white lie, but Secretary Mallory was not going to swallow his pride and call the GDO to help in the search. He understood the President's concern, but reactivating the Reapers was out of the question.

No way, he thinks. *We got rid of that pain-in-the-ass GDO once and now this …*

His assistant, Mrs. Julie Bonnot, knocks and peers into the room. Secretary Mallory spins in his chair, facing the door, and waves her in. She politely drops a folder on his desk.

The label on the front reads:

Global Defense Organization — Confidential

He glances down, opens the front cover and shakes his head in exasperation. He pounds his fist onto the desk and grinds his teeth, total outrage radiates from his entire body.

"Sir?" Mrs. Bonnot says nervously, her hand trembling.

Secretary Mallory waves his hand back and forth dismissively and mouths an apology. He then shoos her out of the room so he can finish with his unpleasant teleconference.

Turning once more to face his wall of awards, Secretary Mallory waits for a pause in the President's rambling and says, "Mr. President, our best technical resources are on the trail of the Aurora's thieves. Honestly speaking, bringing in someone new and completely unfamiliar with the investigation will only slow us down.

We'll have to divert critical resources just to educate them as to our current status. It could set us back days or longer, sir."

There, he thinks. *That ought to be enough to stop the President's whining about the fucking GDO.*

In less than sixty seconds, after listening to the President's response, Secretary Mallory's smugness is replaced by shear frustration. The Secretary's pupils grow larger and larger, then he closes his eyes, puffs out his chin, and slowly shakes his head from side to side.

"And the funding?" Secretary Mallory rudely demands. Then he backs off a bit as he remembers to whom he is speaking.

While listening to the President's final instructions, Secretary Mallory leans back in his chair and brushes the top of his head with his left hand, a final show of defeat.

"Yes, Mr. President. I understand. I have their confidential file right here on my desk. I'll contact Fleet Admiral Wolverine within the hour, sir," Secretary Mallory says. The words alone nearly stick in his throat; he'd almost rather bite off his own tongue than to make that phone call.

If I have to allow those damned cavalier GDO pilots to help with our search for the Aurora, they sure as hell won't get any support from my organization. I will not *be outdone by them again,* Secretary Mallory thinks. *Shit. What a day ...*

After saying their goodbyes and hanging up, Secretary Mallory buzzes Julie. She enters the room, and right away, she can see his eyes glaring with anger. With what, she has no idea. She has been the assistant to Secretary Mallory for the past seven years. Over that time, she has become accustomed to his emotional outbursts. She doesn't care to know what sparked his anger today anymore than she has in the past. She's learned how to work through his outbursts.

She asks quietly, "Is there anything I can do to help, sir?"

Her peaceful personality is an enormous benefit to the Secretary. Numerous times in the past, she was able to encourage him to see the light and reasoning behind decisions that he vehemently opposed. With the wit and skillfulness of an experienced negotiator, Julie's service to Secretary Mallory is invaluable and above reproach.

Trying not to become more agitated, Secretary Mallory says, "Julie. Please contact Fleet Admiral Wolverine at his personal residence."

He hands her the confidential GDO folder and adds, "His number should be in here."

"Right away, sir," she promptly says. "Will that be all? Shall I send him through once I get him on the line?"

"Yes. Send him on through," he replies, feeling resigned to the President's decision. His voice evens out as he says, "I need to speak to Secretary Dow and Colonel Landis after that. Please ring them once I've finished with Admiral Wolverine."

She nods and leaves the room.

A few minutes later, as Secretary Mallory speaks to Admiral Wolverine, Julie heads down to the cafeteria, where she spends at least thirty minutes enjoying a perfect cup of coffee. She does this because her desk is in a position where she can hear the loud conversation between her boss and the leader of the GDO; a conversation she doesn't want to hear, with her boss in his present state of mind.

Two hours later, from his modest but comfortable home in southeastern Michigan, Fleet Admiral Wolverine contacts Admiral PVL in Europe to discuss how to bring the GDO back online. Initially, Wolverine thought he had the wrong number when PVL's daughter, Samantha, answered his private cell phone.

After a brief exchange of greetings, she cheerfully says, "My dad told me I should answer this phone in case he gets an important call. Sorry if it alarmed you."

She explains to Wolverine that her dad has been sick with stomach flu and is temporarily unavailable. From their Naarden, Netherlands apartment, she chats with Wolverine for almost ten minutes until she sees her dad returning from the lavatory.

She races toward him and hands him the phone, telling him, "It's Wolverine on the phone, daddy."

PVL's lanky form seems to be wasting away from his illness … an illness which is lingering and taking a physical toll on him. The graying hair at his temples is now covering more of his head than only a few weeks ago, and his once fierce blue eyes are now droopy and dull.

PVL heads for a chair and in a weak voice says, "Wolve, my friend, how long has it been? Six … seven months? How's retirement?"

Wolverine chuckles in spite of his concern for the health of his friend, and says, "You know I'll never retire. I'm sorry to hear you're sick, but I hope you recover quickly, because your retirement is over. We've been reactivated."

PVL smiles as he listens to Wolverine's enthusiasm. Just hearing the excitement in his voice brings a flow of

renewed energy to PVL's spirit, even in his flu-weakened
state.

"It's great to hear your voice Wolve, really great, and
you know you can always count on me. Got a plan yet?"
PVL says.

The only part of this conversation that is going to be
tough is when PVL tells Wolverine about the intelligence-
gathering mission he sent Doc and Professor on, without
Wolverine's knowledge.

"The President provided us only enough funding to
reactivate the Reaper's Captains and Commanders, and only
one GDO command center. So, since everything is neatly in
one place, I guess we'll all meet in Australia tomorrow." A
moment later, Wolverine says, "Of course, if you're still not
well, we'll set you up remotely. Not an issue."

When PVL says nothing, Wolverine continues,
"Since LiangShan officially turned in his wings for good
once everything fell apart over ten months ago, I'll contact
the remaining twelve Reapers and arrange for appropriate
transportation." Wolverine paces around the room, gathering
files that he has strewn out on his living room floor.

Nervous, PVL tenses his jaw and feels sweat trickle
down his back before he says, "Actually Wolve, there are

only ten Reapers to contact. Doc and Professor are on assignment."

The silence on the phone is intense, so much so that PVL thinks the call has been disconnected. Pulling the cell away from his face, he looks at the phone, then holds it back up to his ear, "Wolve, you still there?"

"On assignment?" Wolverine asks angrily, "what assignment?"

PVL knows he has to divulge the secret mission and that Wolverine will probably hit the roof.

"Yes, Doc and Professor are on assignment, but just hear me out, Wolve."

PVL continues, hoping Wolverine will just listen as he explains, "I was able to secure a small amount of funding from Luo Chuan, the Chinese Premier, to continue our investigation into RAFCO. The funding was to be part of the GDO refinancing plan, but when Elena was assassinated, you emotionally disappeared. I tried many times to talk to you about the money from Luo, but you were inconsolable. I know Elena's death hit you harder than the rest of us. I know you two were close, and shared mutual dreams of world peace and eradicating terrorism.

"So, after a lot of soul searching, I asked Doc and Professor if they wanted to continue working on exposing

RAFCO, but as undercover agents. They agreed, using the cover as disgruntled and disenchanted ex-military pilots. I was hoping RAFCO would ask them to become members, and that we could pick up enough intel to finally expose them to the world's governments."

"Did they succeed?" Wolverine asks, a little less annoyed.

"I don't know." PVL replies.

"What do you mean, you don't know?"

"Wolve, I lost contact with them over six months ago."

"What?" Wolverine sits down on his couch and lowers his head into hands, shielding his eyes. After a few moments, he asks, "PVL, what do you think happened to them? Do you think they're dead?"

"I really don't know. They were supposed to contact me via a secured FTP site at least monthly, but I haven't had any communication from them for over six months. I'm praying that they successfully infiltrated RAFCO and can't contact me for fear of exposing themselves or something like that." PVL wasn't even sure he believed that anymore, but he tried to sound hopeful.

"Then we may have a bigger issue on our hands," Wolverine says, raising his voice. "The primary reason the

GDO was reactivated is to find who stole the Aurora twelve days ago and to help locate its whereabouts."

Now, it was PVL's turn to fall silent. *No,* he thinks. *They couldn't have had anything to do with that.*

His mind rushes with a flurry of scenarios. It could be a coincidence, it could be a cover story while the U.S. government looks for something even more valuable than the Aurora, it could be … Alas, he is overwhelmed with confusion, grief, shame, and sadness that Wolverine might be right. There are only a handful of people in the world he knows that could get into Area 51 undetected. And of those select few, only three could've successfully piloted the Aurora; Doc is one of those three, and the last he'd heard, the other two were basking in the Hawaiian sunshine without a care.

"Wolve, I … I just don't know what to say," PVL says, barely above a whisper. "If they are responsible for stealing the Aurora, I'm sure they had good reason. We need to trust them, like we always have."

"A good reason?" Wolverine blares into the small phone's microphone. "I don't care about the reason. We have rules of conduct that we do not violate. You already broke one by initiating an undercover mission without proper approval, and now you're telling me that our own pilots are possibly responsible for one of the biggest military heists in U.S. history."

Wolverine scowls, gets up and storms into his tiny office. His face is fire engine red. In fact, if he weren't on blood pressure medication, he'd probably be having a heart attack right now. Flipping frantically through files, he finally pulls out a blue folder. He opens it up and flips part way through, until he comes to her photograph — Brooke.

He gazes at her eyes and feels his resolve and strength begin to crumble, remembering how he promised her he would make the world safe again from "the bad men".

Wolverine's only child, Brooke lived in Miami with her mother. Wolverine and Brooke spoke at least once a week on the phone, and many more times during the week by email or text.

Wolverine recalls his exasperation at the younger generation and their addiction to texting. He smiles fondly, remembering how Brooke taught him how to text so they could always be in touch.

As a surprise for her sixteenth birthday, Wolverine purchased an all-inclusive vacation to Paris for Brooke and her mother. He couldn't go, and he certainly didn't want Brooke to go alone, so he spent the extra money for his ex-wife to go. Since there was no animosity between them, Brooke's mother was pleased to accept.

Before the weeklong Paris trip, Brooke decided to visit her dad while he was on leave from the Navy, at the Port of Jebel Ali in the United Arab Emirates (UAE). She planned to spend four days with him in the UAE, before flying to Paris to meet her mother.

On their last day together, they were in a cab heading for the Madinat Jumeirah to enjoy a day of tourist activities, shopping, dining and sightseeing. While at a stop light, behind a local city bus, a suicide bomber exploded inside the bus. The next thing Wolverine knew, he woke up in the local military hospital. The blast had killed everyone aboard the bus, and a few close by, including the driver of their cab. By some miracle, both Wolverine and Brooke survived.

However, while Wolverine suffered only minor burns and a few cracked ribs, Brooke was in critical condition with a head injury. He was allowed only short visits with her, because the doctors had her on massive amounts of drugs to try to manage her injury. It was during one of those visits with her, that his life-long anti-terrorist commitment began.

Two days after the blast, alarms and buzzers went off, and the hospital staff rushed into Brooke's room. They immediately took her into emergency surgery for severe brain swelling. She didn't make it out of the operating room alive. She died on the table, with the surgeon's hand frantically trying to relieve the pressure, while another doctor tried to revive her.

Wolverine's life was in shambles as he tried to deal with the death of his beloved daughter.

Hearing PVL say his name, Wolverine snaps out of his stupor. He looks down at the image of her lovely face and a sad, yet warm smile softens his face. *Thanks Brooke,* Wolverine thinks. *I needed your help to keep me focused on what really matters.*

"PVL," Wolverine says, with renewed authority. "Our orders from the President are to find the Aurora and return it. If that's not possible, then we are ordered to destroy it. So, based upon what you're telling me, chances are high that Doc and Professor had something to do with its theft. And, if they did," he takes a deep breath, letting it out slowly, "I will support and take responsibility for our Reapers in the field, just like I always have."

PVL thinks, *Yes, I knew you'd come around, Wolve.*

Wolverine continues, "I guess the question we need to answer now is; where did they take it?"

"Right," PVL replies. "I'll work up a prioritization list tonight of potential landings sites that would have easy access to methane fuel, concealed hangers, and a runway system capable of supporting the Aurora. I don't think this damned flu bug is going to allow me to travel for at least another day, possibly two or more. So, once Captains Red Diamond and Viral have finished bringing the Reaper network back online, Wolve, I'll upload my data to you."

"Sounds like a good plan. Say hi to Samantha for me, and keep yourself well-hydrated, my friend. I won't keep you any longer. Kick that flu bug and I'll talk to you again very soon," Wolverine says with the same spunk and energy he had when the GDO was first approved by NATO+ almost six years ago.

Wolverine gets up, closes the folder, and carefully places it into his cabinet for safekeeping. He walks into the main part of the house, and heads for the back door. He opens it and steps out onto the patio. Scanning the horizon first, he then looks up into the sky, locating the still visible crescent outline of the moon.

An enthusiastic grin brightens his face as he says with vigor, "**The Reapers are back!**"

Reaper Two-Six
Year 6

Chapter 13
Iunctus Nos Lucror
Carnarvon, Western Australia

Over the next thirty-six hours, all ten reactivated Reapers and Wolverine arrive at the GDO command center in Carnarvon, Western Australia. As is customary to protect his Reapers from possible threats, Wolverine uses many different airline carriers when arranging transportation. For this gathering, a maximum of two Reapers were on any one flight.

Wolverine has assumed overall command; PVL is still home with the stomach flu, while Loz has been unreachable. *He must be on a cruise in the middle of the Atlantic,* Wolverine thinks while envisioning Loz having a cold beer at an outdoor bar on a Norwegian Cruise Line ship. *Some days, I wish I could join him. But, today is not one of those days. Today is the beginning of the end for RAFCO, if I have anything to do with it.* His thoughts are full of determination.

Today's sunrise marks the fourteenth day since the theft of the Aurora. Commander Blast, up early as usual, decides to get some initial aircraft housecleaning out of the way.

One of the best pilots in Reaper Two-Six, Blast has not always had such a well-respected reputation. For almost half his military flight school training, Blast's kill-to-death ratio rated as the lowest of his class; a rude reminder about the importance of checking his six, especially in close combat quarters, where the enemy's aircraft cannons are deadly. At the end of one particularly humiliating 0-for-22 training day, he vowed he would never allow anyone to sneak up on him again.

DaXx, now a Captain with the Reapers, was one of the assistant flight instructors. He took Blast under his wing and to the amazement of his squad mates, Blast made an almost immediate reversal, eventually graduating with honors. Blast even became one of the most feared pilots of his squadron. This was the beginning of Blast and DaXx's friendship.

After a quick shower, Blast runs his hands through his sandy, somewhat unruly hair, and catches a quick glimpse of himself in the mirror.

It'll have to do, he thinks. His appealing and almost boyish looks conceal the knowledgeable, fearsome pilot inside.

He throws on some grungy clothes thinking, *they're only going to get grimy and stinky anyway.*

Reaper Two-Six
Year 6

Smirking, he mutters to himself, "Hell, Wolverine doesn't care. He's not much for formal military attire anyway, unless we're meeting some pretentious diplomat."

Around the command centers, Wolverine always dresses casually in khaki pants and a comfortable shirt, but never loses the appearance of being in charge and in control. By his relaxed appearance and youthful-looking face, you would never know Wolverine is a U.S. Navy Admiral veteran with many years' combat experience.

Blast walks through the main control room and exits through the door closest to the hanger. He scampers down the metal stairs and heads over to the far end. He smacks the yellow button on the wall and hears the squeak and grind of the large bay doors opening. The soothing, morning air starts to invade the stuffiness of the vast hanger.

"Ah," Blast sighs.

He proceeds to pull the covers off the canopy, inlet and exhaust on all the aircraft requested by Wolverine: the X-47s, E/A-18Gs, F-35s and F-22s. Folding the covers neatly, he stacks them on the stainless steel racks. Next, the protective sheathings on the aircrafts' sensors are slipped off and placed into their respective storage bins. Finally, the ground power cables are snapped into place so that each aircraft's electronics can be individually verified through a set of preflight checks.

"Don't need any surprises up there," Blast mumbles.

As more of the Reapers join Blast in the hanger, the enormous task of setting up the command center begins.

By late afternoon, the Reaper network is operational except for two of the servers, which are still down with hard-drive and router failures.

My guess is that it will be at least another couple of days until I find replacement parts for those babies, Captain Red Diamond muses. *What are you going to do? That's what happens when you mothball electronics; they misbehave when you bring them back to life.*

Red Diamond sets up PVL with a new network ID and password since they'd previously removed all the old access codes for security reasons. As he clicks to send the email, Wolverine steps over to his workstation and sits down.

"I need you to activate Doc and Professor's GPS beacons," Wolverine says.

For a moment, Red Diamond simply stares at his commander, trying to process the order thoroughly, and hoping he just didn't understand what he is asking; but Wolverine does not waver.

"You know what that will do, right?" Red Diamond asks. "If we activate their sensors, and they are still under cover, it could expose them."

Wolverine nods, "I know what it means; but if Doc and Professor did take the Aurora, the situation is volatile, and we need to take control immediately. To do that, we need to know where they are."

Red Diamond nods slowly. He looks over at his computer screen and types in the commands to bring the obscure folder into view. After several password protected entries, he slides the keyboard toward Wolverine, who will type in the final code needed to activate the sensors.

Wolverine hesitates a few seconds, then types in his authorization code, and presses the Enter key. They wait in silence, watching the screen for confirmation that the activation was successful. One minute goes by, then two, then three … finally Red Diamond shakes his head.

"I'm not sure what this means, sir, but it's not picking up anything."

Wolverine's mouth forms a thin straight line. Then he says, "Keep it looping through a ping every minute or so. They have either masked the devices somehow, or they're dead and buried so deep underground we'll never find them."

Reaper Two-Six
Year 6

He stands up to leave, and then adds, "But one way or another, we've got to find them."

Red Diamond watches Wolverine walk away, then turns toward the monitor to set up the steady ping, hoping for the first option Wolverine suggested, not the second one. "Come on Doc and Professor," he says trying to coax the signal to appear. He pleads again, looking at the steady pulse of the radar type ping on the monitor. "Show us you're still alive."

At the far end of the hanger, six X-47 remotely piloted stealth drones are nearly ready; they've been cleaned, the preflight checks have been performed, their infrared and thermal imaging systems are operational, and they have been fitted with two extended range underbelly fuel tanks. Once verified that the sensor array dome under the aircraft's nose can communicate properly with the Reaper network, the aircraft will be cleared for flight.

The X-47 is a single engine, all composite, tailless aircraft primarily designed for aerial reconnaissance. As no pilot accommodations are required, the aircraft is only a few feet deep in the center, giving the small flying wing-shaped aircraft superb stealth characteristics. With a wing span of sixty-two feet and a length of thirty-eight feet, it also has excellent long range performance.

Reaper Two-Six
Year 6

In the central part of the hanger, four E/A-18Gs, four F-35s and four F-22s are still many hours away from being fully equipped and available. The fitting of appropriate missile, bomb and electronic countermeasure armament is very time consuming, and attention to detail is critical.

The three fuel trucks finish topping-off all eighteen aircraft then leave the hanger through the automatic service door. Because the facility has been unused for so long, the trucks need to refill in anticipation of future missions. After reaching the far end of the five-mile long base, the trucks pass through the electronic security point, to commence their thirty-minute drive to the Carnarvon Municipal Airport for a much-needed fill-up.

As Wolverine requested, Red Diamond is the acting second in command, until PVL is well enough to resume full duties. After a long, busy day, the afternoon gives way to twilight; Red Diamond walks out onto the hanger's upper stairway platform, cups his hands around his mouth, and loudly announces to the Reapers on the hanger floor, "I've synced the uplink server with the network, so we're ready. Get the X-47's communications tested and verified, pronto."

To insure everything is mission ready, a live video stream from each X-47's sensor array dome is performed. The imaging system pivots through two full circles, once with the infrared and once with the thermal camera. Red Diamond and Viral are in the command center's master control station monitoring the flow of information from all six aircraft.

A few tense minutes pass as the automated array domes spin through their preprogrammed movements. Both Red Diamond and Viral meticulously watch the data — no dropouts are allowed in order for the aircraft to be approved for flight.

Finally, Viral opens the door to the hanger and calls out, "Perfect! Nicely done everyone. I'll be right down for the final inspection, then we'll give them the stamp of approval."

Many years ago, Wolverine established a mandatory second preflight inspection for each aircraft, performed by a different Reaper other than the assigned pilot. The additional inspection was intended to protect the pilot and the success of the mission. Wolverine witnessed many accidents during his career that were simply due to issues that an extra check would have caught.

A few minutes later, an ovation of cheers erupts from within the hanger; the X-47s have passed inspection!

Hearing the celebratory atmosphere in the hanger, Wolverine, Red Diamond, and the remaining Reapers in the command center join the applause on the upper platform. Wolverine beams with joy and excitement. He takes a step up onto one of the railing crossbars, so everyone can see him clearly.

He shares a smile and, with much elation, says, "My friends, I am honored to be in your presence and humbled by your dedication and courage. The Reapers are not just a group of top notch pilots and covert mission specialists, but a devout family with a common goal; to make the world a safer place to live.

"The past few months have been tough on all of us, and I am personally sorry for letting you all down. However, today I ask that you not dwell in the past, but on the mission at hand.

"I am grateful that each of you decided to be a part of the Reapers again, giving us another chance to free the world from the chains of terrorism. This is an excellent opportunity to show the world how valuable we are.

"Because of your outstanding efforts today, Reaper Two-Six is officially reinstated." He raises both hands high above his head, clenches his fists, and shakes his arms from front to back thinking, *Yes, we're finally back!*

The Reapers explode with cheers and excitement; whistling, clapping, high-fiving, fist bumping, chest bumping, and even stomping on the medal platform, nearly shaking it loose from its mounts. All Wolverine can do is smile and take in the moment. For very soon, the evil that is RAFCO will be his entire focus.

Once the festivity begins to subside, Wolverine steps down from the railing, points at Viral, and makes a swinging motion with his arm. Viral understands and unleashes a piercing whistle; the high pitched shrill ricochets off the hanger's walls before penetrating everyone's ears, sending uncontrollable shivers down their spines.

"Chow time," Viral bellows.

While his Reapers enjoy a hearty meal, Wolverine returns to the command center and settles into a more secluded adjoining room. Grabbing his laptop, he sits in the comfortable La-Z-Boy chair and opens a file from PVL. *I hope he's feeling better,* he thinks.

Beginning to review PVL's recommendations, Wolverine's eyes, squinting to focus, lock onto the screen with hawk-like intensity. Using the touchpad, he slowly scrolls through the document, occasionally mumbling aloud, "Hmmm, ah, yes, good idea."

Once he is finished reading, he slouches deeper into the plush seat and shuts the computer lid. Wolverine takes some time to allow the data to cement itself; melding all available intel into a cohesive picture and action plan.

Hearing the commotion of activity downstairs in the mess hall brings another smile to his face. *I'm grateful to be back,* he thinks. *I've missed this.*

After a few minutes, he raises his head and slowly nods while thinking of the Reaper motto:

Iunctus Nos Lucror (United We Win).

And this time ... we shall *win.*

Chapter 14
Infallible Storm

After dinner, the Reapers head upstairs, to the main control room, for the upcoming briefing.

Damn impressive! Commander Magic thinks, stretching his neck to get a better look at the vast array of electronic intelligence in the room.

LCD screens of every imaginable size are mounted to the walls and sitting on desks. The displays show satellite imagery from around the world, depicting current weather conditions, mission details, potential targets, and a lot of information Magic can only guess at. There are also icons pinpointing fuel, weapons and aircraft status, along with what he thinks might be U.S. and NATO+ military locations. The large sixty-five-inch screen on the far wall appears to show color coded military movements in green, blue, purple, red and orange symbols. Color, data, and information bombard his brain from all directions.

Magic jabs Commander Cloud in the ribs, then points across the room at the big screen, and says, "I wonder if Wolverine was able to get satellite TV reinstalled."

Deciding to razz Cloud about his precious "football" team, Magic says, "I hear Greece is the team to beat in

Europe. Wouldn't it be sweet to watch them take it to England on that beautiful screen? It would almost be like being there."

Cloud narrows his eyes and offers Magic a symbolic gesture; he flicks his hand out from under his chin implying, *fuck off.*

A few of the Reapers sitting near Magic and Cloud overhear their conversation; after seeing Cloud's gesture, the room explodes into animated banter and raucous laughter.

From the adjoining room, Wolverine shakes his head and grins, thinking, *They're competitive to the very end. It's all in good fun, though.*

In their hearts, he knows they would give their lives to save a fellow Reaper. He continues to remind himself how grateful he is to have such a perfectly bonded group.

He grabs his laptop and heads for the door.

Wolverine walks down the hall and steps into the main control room. Without any prompting from him, the voices start to subside as he takes a seat at the end of the room closest to the big screen. As there are only ten Reapers instead of the usual forty-eight, he motions everyone to huddle around so they can easily talk and share ideas.

I might as well get this out of the way, Wolverine thinks. *The part about Doc and Professor is going to give them quite a shock, I imagine.*

He takes a sip of water, clears his throat and begins: "Reapers, our mission is to locate, recover and return the U.S. military's top secret hypersonic aircraft, the Aurora." He knows many or maybe even all these pilots know of its existence, but because of the multinational nature of the Reapers, he's not leaving anything to chance.

He waits a moment, until the shock settles down throughout the room. He hears several comments nearby.

"Is he serious?"

"Come on? You must be kidding?"

"What happened to it?"

"Stolen, or was it lost?"

"No way, the Aurora?"

When the chatter dies down, he continues, "It's believed that the Aurora has fallen into combative hands; quite possibly our old 'friends,' RAFCO."

Once more murmurs circle through the room. Whistles of surprise bounce off the walls.

Wolverine adds, "If the return of the aircraft is not possible, then we are ordered to destroy it as a last resort. The President of the United States has classified this as a national security threat due to its technical equipment and advanced stealth capabilities.

"Fourteen days ago, two individuals flew the Aurora out of Area 51 and survived a barrage of twelve missiles fired by Nellis' scrambled jets."

"Holy shit!" Captain Ranger blurts. Realizing his sudden outburst has interrupted the Commander, he adds, "Sorry sir."

Wolverine smiles and says, "Those were my sentiments exactly, which brings me to the next point. PVL and I believe that Doc and Professor may be the two who are responsible for stealing the Aurora."

The stillness in the air is so quiet the faint whirling sound of the computer cooling fans can be heard.

Yeah, I figured that might be their reaction, Wolverine thinks. *I'd be shocked, too, if I were in their position. How often does someone tell you that your squad mates could be responsible for treason?*

He presses forward, saying, "Because of my distraught behavior at the collapse of the GDO funding and the death of the president of NATO+, PVL felt compelled to keep the spirit of the Reapers alive as long as possible, hoping to finally bring an end to RAFCO's world-wide tyrannical regime.

"It was his hope that Doc and Professor could uncover enough evidence to finally expose RAFCO for what they really are: a danger to world stability … an infection that needs to be eradicated. Doc and Professor were sent deep undercover, but without the standard GDO electronic and support network. So, at this time …" Wolverine takes a deep breath and swallows hard, feeling sadness in his heart to have to report this to his friends. "Their whereabouts are unknown."

The blank stares on the Reapers' faces tell the whole story, and Wolverine senses their pain, confusion and concern.

Summoning the strength to put positive momentum into their activities, Wolverine says, "I want to find Doc and Professor alive as much as anyone. We are all family. But, we must not fail our mission to prevent the Aurora from being used for malicious purposes. So, we've decided to focus our attention on the following RAFCO sites with the strongest possibility of harboring the Aurora: One, RAFCO HQ in southwestern Colombia; two, Tanzania in eastern Africa; and three, Ukraine in Eastern Europe."

Wolverine opens his laptop and, after a few button taps, the large LCD screen displays a global map, with the three RAFCO sites highlighted in red.

Standing up and directing a laser pointer at the screen, he explains the plan for the forthcoming mission, saying, "Two X-47s will fly-over and remain near each location, insuring almost constant coverage. There is a risk of detection, but the greater risk of not finding the Aurora grows more perilous with each passing day. Therefore, we will take any necessary risks to find the Aurora, thereby achieving our goal.

"With visual, infrared and thermal imaging systems onboard the drones, I want to locate the Aurora, or at least have strong indications of its whereabouts within the next twenty-four to thirty-six hours."

"Red Diamond," Wolverine says.

"Sir," Red Diamond replies.

"Commanders Fox and Gunner," Wolverine announces.

"Yes sir," the commanders respond in unison.

Feeling the power of the moment, Wolverine looks into their eyes and says, "You're my best X-47 pilots. I am entrusting the three of you to find the Aurora and, hopefully, Doc and Professor as well. Make us proud, gentlemen."

"Sir. Yes sir!" they all reply in unison.

Wolverine nods and turns his attention to the remaining seven pilots. "I have decided to finish what we started a year ago," he says. "I want the RAFCO bases around the world leveled. A previous commander of mine, now a Navy Rear Admiral in charge of the Carrier Strike Group One fleet, has given us permission to base our operations from the USS Carl Vinson.

"The Vinson is currently sailing in the eastern Pacific and awaits your arrival. From here on out, Captain Viral is in command of the Storm Reapers Squadron. Once Red Diamond and I determine that a specific RAFCO base is not hiding the Aurora or holding Doc and Professor, the Storm Reapers will launch a full one-pass strike and level the camp."

Wolverine closes the laptop, stands, and finishes his briefing, saying, "You are the world's most elite squadron. We were joined together to make a difference, to bring safety and security to the world, and to allow people to live without fear. I am proud of each of you, and I'm honored to have you as members of Reaper Two-Six."

He places his hand, palm down, in the middle of the circle of Reapers as a quarterback might do just before breaking a huddle. Each pilot follows, placing their hand on top of the next. Wolverine looks around, sees their intensity, their focus, their energy, and the passion in their eyes.

Reaper Two-Six
Year 6

In a commanding voice, he simply says, "Make us proud." They all raise their hands and continue the energy with high fives.

Just over an hour later, 2100 local time, all six X-47s taxi to the main runway and hold position, awaiting the official signal to begin operation Infallible Storm.

"In position, sir," Red Diamond says.

Under normal operations, each X-47 is remotely piloted by a Reaper at a single control station, typically located along the back wall of the main command center room. Each remote Reaper pilot wears a headset while continuously watching a live video feed from the aircraft's front and side navigational cameras, displayed on three LCD screens before him.

The center screen contains a military style heads-up-display (HUD), so the remote pilot focuses most of his attention on this screen. The side screens display a multitude of auxiliary information that best suits the individual pilot and specific mission; a moving map, engine health information, fuel status, even the position, speed, altitude, heading, and attitude of up to four additional X-47s, typically used for close formation flying or for in-air refueling operations.

Reaper Two-Six
Year 6

As with all stealth missions, no radar transmissions are ever allowed. The secured flight control data that streams from the X-47 contains the most current GPS information imbedded within it. The receiving dish arrays on the north side of the GDO command center relays the aircraft signals to the appropriate flight control station.

Sitting in his chair at the master control center station, Wolverine scans the vast array of monitors directly in front of him. A few seconds later, after analyzing the video feed data from all X-47s, he nods and announces over the comm system, "Cleared for takeoff."

The X-47's engines spool up to maximum power, emitting just the slightest whine, then rush down the runway, lifting off the ground with amazing grace. A few seconds later, the X-47s split-up, heading for the three RAFCO locations around the world.

Wolverine reaches out and carefully picks up his extra large cup of coffee. After a quick blow across the rim, he enjoys a hefty swallow of the extra rich mocha flavor.

I sure hope my guys are up for this, he ponders. *I've never had one pilot controlling two X-47s before.*

With the limited financial resources given to the reinstated GDO, Wolverine had to be enormously creative in order to cover the most ground in the shortest time and with the fewest pilots. Even with only three pilots controlling the X-47s, it leaves merely seven for the manned missions.

It'll have to do, he reasons. *It's on me to locate the needle in the haystack ... I can't let them down, no matter what I have to do to support them.* Wolverine will need to weed through all the visual, infrared and thermal surveillance data for all six X-47s; a daunting task for one man.

With the start of the X-47's missions, the seven Reapers are left with an extremely long night ahead; finishing the armament, verifying the electronics, and performing preflight checks on all remaining aircraft: F-22s, F-35s and E/A-18Gs.

Down on the hanger floor, Commander Blast glares at his fellow Reapers and bellows, "Why didn't *I* get picked for a cushy job?"

Captain Pop chimes in, barking, "Man, those dudes get all the breaks. While we're busting our asses trying to get the real planes ready for tomorrow, there're upstairs in their plush seats playing video games. Oh, I suppose they want you to believe that they're 'piloting' those RC toys. Yeah, right. Hell, I could sleepwalk and fly that X-47 bitch."

Muffled laughter, a few *you got that right,* and hand slaps are heard around the hanger.

Reaper Two-Six
Year 6

With the X-47s now passing through twenty thousand feet and on their way to their long range cruise altitude of forty-two thousand feet, Wolverine can now direct his focus elsewhere for the next few hours. Ever since PVL was granted access to the newly revived Reaper network, he has been slowly collecting satellite imagery. With two servers down, there is limited disc space, and the communication bandwidth is significantly reduced.

PVL has been carefully and quietly discussing the Aurora situation with his old buddy from the Dutch military, Nicholas Corrigan. Nic is director of the Natural Environment Research Council Radar (NERC) facility in Aberystwyth, United Kingdom. PVL is intimately aware of Nic's tenacity for all types of atmospheric monitoring techniques. In fact, Nic's expertise provided the GDO with critical information and even hardware to support a high visibility mission almost a year ago.

PVL hopes that Nic might devise a method to see the Aurora's flight path, because there is a significant chance that if RAFCO senses someone is closing in on them, they might suddenly launch a strike or decide to move the aircraft to a different location. Being able to track the Aurora in-flight could be critical to the mission.

Wolverine opens the secured folder system and dives into the initial material from PVL; all the while thinking about the two Reapers who are unaccounted for, Doc and Professor.

God be with you two, Wolverine thinks solemnly. *I sure hope you are both okay.*

Chapter 15
Redemption Begins
RAFCO HQ, Colombia

Holy shit, they're here! Doc thinks. She tries to conceal her anxiety and mounting fear, hoping it won't be visible.

Professor, Doc and the Marquez brothers stand up and walk to the edge of the RAFCO HQ's rooftop patio. In the distance, a mass of associates follows two large crates on trailers moving toward them. The Reapers can sense the celebratory atmosphere and enthusiasm, even four stories up and over a mile away.

Whistles, singing, and all manner of body animations emanate from the crowd around the crates, drowning out the diesel truck's engine straining to pull the trailer.

Doc's face goes pale, and an uncontrollable tightness grips her stomach, nearly causing her to vomit. She reaches for the ledge, trying to steady herself in hopes of keeping her breakfast from coming up. Without warning, her muscles go limp, and she tumbles to the hard concrete floor in a panic attack.

This is my fault ... This is my fault ... This is my fault, she repeats over again through her mind. Her entire body is now in a type of epileptic seizure, shaking out of control.

The Marquez brothers pay her no attention as their minds are aligned with their fellow associates; celebrating the beginning of the RAFCO revolution.

Professor drops to his knees, wanting to hug Doc to comfort her. His heart explodes in pain to see her in such distress. *I told her it's not her fault.*

"Shh, it's okay," he whispers. "We'll fix this."

For the past three days, the Reapers have been isolated from the camp's normal activity, with minimal explanation. They have spent those days either locked in their room or sitting on the rooftop patio with armed guards.

Esteban made it sound like it was a reward for all their hard work, some relaxing time off, but the Reapers didn't believe it. When Professor finally pressed him, Esteban simply smiled and said, "Trust me. Your work and dedication to us will not go unnoticed."

Bullshit, Professor thinks, recalling Esteban's words. *Has he made us and is just waiting to kill us after he launches the attack? Does he want us to suffer, knowing that our actions could kill millions and possibly lead to a world calamity?*

Reaper Two-Six
Year 6

Slowly and gingerly embracing Doc, Professor desperately tries to calm her down. He slides his hand under her chin and lifts her head upward. They lock eyes; her anguish is overwhelmingly clear. He pulls her closer and whispers into her ear. "It's not your fault. Please believe me … Please …"

Suddenly realizing they're alone, "Where'd they …" Carlos says just as Miguel taps him on the shoulder and points toward Professor and Doc huddled on the floor.

They rush to the Reapers to try to find out what's going on. Professor decides it's best if he can get some time alone with Doc in hopes that she'll snap out of her anxiety, or whatever she's feeling, so he makes up a story.

"She has a stomach bug. Maybe something she ate this morning."

Professor asks, "Can you help me get her back to our suite? She really needs to lie down."

The brothers nod after seeing Doc's ghostly white complexion. They slowly bring Doc to her feet, but her wobbly knees will not yet support even her small frame. Professor motions to Carlos and then slips Doc's left arm over his shoulders; Carlos does the same for the right side. They both carefully wrap their free hand around her mid-section. Miguel leads the way, unlocking doors and holding them open while they ease Doc down the four flights of stairs and across the runway to the Reaper's suite.

Carefully, they guide Doc onto her bed, elevating her head with pillows and slipping off her boots. Miguel grabs a water bottle from the refrigerator, twists the top off, and offers it to Doc. She glances at him, and for the first time since they arrived, Doc is grateful for the Marquez brother's attentiveness.

"Thank you," she says in a weak, raspy voice.

The sounds from outside begin to grow louder, drawing the brother's attention. Professor tries to use this to their advantage and says, "I wouldn't want to keep you from missing the celebration. Don't worry, I'll take good care of her this afternoon. Go, enjoy … we'll be fine."

Carlos and Miguel quietly exchange a few words in Spanish. The expressions on their faces clearly show they are concerned about leaving the Reapers alone. Miguel's eyes dart around the room, while Carlos seems focused on the festivities outside.

After uttering a few more words, and a final look around the room, the brothers decide to leave Doc and Professor alone. They turn and head for the door. After exiting and pushing the door firmly closed, the Reapers hear the sound of the deadbolt sliding into the wall, locking them inside.

Professor places his ear firmly against the door until he is certain that both brothers have left the building.

I don't believe it, he thinks. *They actually left us unguarded, and they probably won't be checking on us for quite a while because of the festivities. This is my chance. I have to do it now!*

The Reapers have been debating the past three days, trying to formulate a plan to get word to PVL. Realizing that Doc is not up to it yet, Professor decides to seize the moment; with firm conviction, he whispers into her ear and heads for the window.

Doc summons the strength to sit upright, snaps her head toward him, and is only able to get out, "No!" but it's too late; he pops the glass out of the frame and climbs through the window.

Gone ... she thinks, before putting her arm over her eyes to shut out the light.

Once down on the ground, Professor takes refuge in the nearby shrubs and quickly scans the surrounding area. Tall, spiked grass and weeds on the edges of the runway lead into the woods farther back. Some rolling mounds of dirt, a few military vehicles, and various buildings of different sizes separate him from his objective — the Aurora's hanger.

Professor hunkers down on his stomach, trying to see if there are guards posted outside the hanger. He crawls forward on his elbows to the front of the building. Carefully, using the uncut tufts of tall grass as cover, he looks around the corner, focusing on the hanger doors over a thousand yards away. The mid-afternoon sun makes the insects active, and he has to resist swiping at flies, ants and gnats as he raises his body a little higher to see over a small hill.

Nope, I can't tell. I'll just have to make do; been through a hell of a lot tighter spots than this steamy pathetic excuse for a camp, he ponders.

He watches the truck carrying the missile crates turn onto the far end of the runway. *Better get moving,* he thinks. *I don't have much time.*

He doubles back and, after moving around to the rear of their building, takes off running. Looking like a giant praying mantis, he quickly scampers from vehicle-to-vehicle and then building-to-building, blending in with the surrounding environment as much as possible. The final twenty yards prove to be the most grueling as he inches his way closer to the edge of the tall grass in front of the runway, directly across from the Aurora's hanger.

Reaper Two-Six
Year 6

His forehead, now soaked with salty sweat, drips directly into his eyes. He squeezes them shut and blinks rapidly, hoping the burning sensation will pass soon.

Flattening as low as he can get, he slides his arms forward and slowly separates a few blades of grass, scouting out the hanger's surrounding area.

"One ... two ... three ... umm ... Shit! ... Four ... five ... Fuck!" he whispers, gritting his teeth harder with each number.

He pulls his arms back, tucking them under his chin, allowing the grass to fully conceal his position once more.

Closing his eyes, he says in an inaudible whisper, "Think, Professor ... Think."

A three-dimensional image of the hanger begins to materialize in his mind. He places purple dots at the approximate locations of the five RAFCO associates, drops in a mental picture of the Aurora and then a few key additional items take shape; the desk, the rear door, the side door, storage racks, and the back room where a few pieces of extraneous equipment, like forklifts, are kept. His eyes roll around under his eyelids as he mentally walks through an action plan. After a few seconds, his eyes pop open ... *Got it.*

Knowing he has only minutes before the mass of RAFCO associates are too close, he swiftly rambles along the runway, still hidden within the weeds. Finally exiting the grassy area, he sneaks behind a methane fuel truck. With his heart pounding so fiercely that his hands begin to shake, he psychs himself up and sprints across the runway.

Having no idea if anyone saw him, he pushes forward thinking, *No turning back now anyway. I might as well not worry about something I can't change.*

He scampers his way rapidly to the back of the hanger and carefully opens the side door; checking to locate the RAFCO associates.

His eyes widen: *Thank God.* They have all moved toward the front of the hanger, watching their prized missiles make their way down the runway.

Professor slips inside the back part of the hanger and spots the laptop. He grabs it, along with a few extra goodies lying around he thinks might come in handy. He exits the building and rockets back across the runway, sliding behind a fuel truck.

The emotional and physical fatigue is starting to drain him, so he pauses to take a few deep breaths, while pondering his next move. *I'd better take the long way back, but not too long because there's no telling when they'll discover the computer is gone. We need to be out of here for good within the hour, if not sooner.*

Reaper Two-Six
Year 6

Professor darts out from behind the truck, keeping as low to the ground as possible. More than halfway to the woods, his toe catches a dip in the uneven ground, tripping him and almost causing him to fall face-first into the dirt. His reflexes from his younger years playing running back save him from potential injury and almost certain severe damage to his valuable possession — the laptop with the images from Esteban's room that reveal RAFCO's deadly plans.

After a few more seconds, he finally crosses the threshold of the dense woods. He continues for another thirty feet deeper into the woods, before settling to the ground behind a large tree. If he was back in his home state, Professor would marvel at such an amazing plant and would probably Google the local flora to find out what genus it was; but here, all he can do is spare a single glance at the beautiful tree and be thankful that it is big enough to conceal him.

He looks around the base of the trunk, checking to see if he was followed.

"Alright, let's do this," he says while opening the laptop and pushing the power button. The warm glow of the screen illuminates his face in the darkened, wooded area.

Once the Windows operating system finishes booting, he opens the FTP program and locates the folder containing all the image files taken by Doc in Esteban's room.

Reaper Two-Six
Year 6

Seventy-eight ... Yup, that's all of them, he thinks.
Oh, I should really add a special "read me" or "important"
file that explains our general conclusions; a brief summary
of our intel. It shouldn't take but a minute or two anyway.

He opens a text editor program and proceeds to type
quickly. A few minutes later, he saves the file in the same
location as Doc's images.

"There," he says. "Seventy-nine total files, all nicely
packed into one folder, ready for delivery to the GDO."

He sighs ... *At least it used to be the GDO.*

In the FTP program's remote site area, he types in
PVL's private secure site code information. Suddenly his
thoughts drift toward Doc, and he wonders if he'll be able to
get her out of the suite safely, because once he presses Enter,
the clock really starts ticking; they'll be completely exposed
to RAFCO as undercover spies. It's just a matter of time
before they figure it out and come for them, guns blazing.

Without warning, a snap resonates from behind him.
Instinctually, he grabs the knife he stole from the Aurora's
hanger and in one quick, and smooth motion, he slides the
laptop off his legs and spins his body toward the left,
reaching behind the tree. He stops short and in a startled
voice says, "Doc?"

Reaper Two-Six
Year 6

Professor stands up and reaches over to give her a hug. But, instead of returning the embrace, she punches him in the stomach; not too hard, but hard enough that he'll remember it for a while.

"Oof!" he manages to say.

"Next time, don't you dare go alone on a mission like that again, or I'll kill you myself," Doc snaps.

"Nice to see you too," he says jokingly, gasping for air. He sits back on the ground and says seriously, "No. Actually, I'm glad to see you. This'll be perfect."

He takes a few deep breaths and exhales slowly, hoping to ease the pain shooting up both sides of his abdomen. Finally, he looks up at her, reaches over, and hands her the laptop.

Seeing the FTP program loaded, she asks, "How did you know it was possible to use this computer to access PVL's site?"

"Yesterday, I overheard our 'pleasant' airplane mechanic, Pancho, bellowing as usual. Only this time, he actually said something useful." Professor chuckles before adding, "I heard him say 'It take four fucking hours on Internet to find goddamn temperature sensor. Fucking Americans, everything must be special. Now, you want me find mounting rack for underbelly hard points? You're crazy.' Then the rest trailed off into a bickering session. I reasoned that if he can access the Internet outside of the camp, then I was betting we could access PVL's site."

Doc smacks him on the shoulder and right side of the face saying, "You risked us getting killed on a hunch? What the fuck?"

Professor shrugs and says, "We had to do something. I'm guessing they'll be mission ready with the missiles and the Aurora within the next twelve to eighteen hours, depending on how good our pal, Pancho, is.

"I'm sorry for leaving you, but it was time to risk it all, and you were in no condition to go. It was our only hope of redeeming ourselves and saving society as we know it.

"I bet they've made us anyway, and were just torturing us emotionally; hoping we'd break down and maybe even talk once we saw the fully loaded Aurora roar into the sky on its first mission."

Doc simply nods in understanding and acknowledgment. She reaches down and smacks the laptop's Enter key, watching the files begin to rapidly transfer.

Three minutes later, she says, "It's done. Now, let's get the fuck out of here."

Reaper Two-Six
Year 6

Chapter 16
Displaced

"You fucking imbeciles!" Esteban shouts at his second in command, Fernando. "I knew something wasn't right with those two. And now they are gone ... poof! Like los serpientes in the night!" He slams his fists on the table and inadvertently hits a loose nail, increasing his mindless rage.

At the same time, lightening flashes across the sky. This seems to soothe Esteban, as if the weather is in agreement with his anger. Thunder rattles the loose glass in the window frame, and Esteban glances at the window briefly, before returning his attention to Fernando and the matter at hand.

Fernando's face is flushed with anger and embarrassment. After all, it was on his approval that the Marquez brothers brought the Americans to the camp. Now his ass is on the line because of their fuck up.

The Marquez brothers! Fernando realizes he has to turn this around before Esteban decides he's involved in a conspiracy.

He clears his throat and speaks with absolute certainty, "The Marquez brothers are behind this, Esteban."

Esteban turns around and glares at Fernando. "You approved their recommendation, Fernando." He pounds his chest with his fist, "And I trusted your decision. What does that mean, huh? Am I to believe you are not trustworthy?"

Esteban moves toward his desk, where Fernando knows a 9mm pistol lays hidden in the top desk drawer. He knows he has only one chance to plead his case and to pin this whole mess on the Marquez brothers.

"You're right, sir, but the Marquez brothers were the ones to have all the face-to-face meetings with them. I trusted them to have covered all the bases. Obviously, I chose the wrong men for the job." Fernando knows that a small admittance of guilt is good, it relieves Esteban from any wrong-doing; but he also knows the majority of the guilt needs to rest on someone else's shoulders or he could face the muzzle end of that 9mm pistol himself. "Trust me, I will make this right. I will bring these bastards to justice."

Esteban glares at Fernando with narrowed eyes. "Can I trust you?" he asks.

Fernando unsnaps his holster and growls, "Yes sir. I'll take care of those idiots, then I'll go after the fucking Americans myself."

Reaper Two-Six
Year 6

The look on Esteban's face tells Fernando he bought some time, so he quickly leaves his boss, striding with a purpose toward the Marquez brother's quarters.

After Fernando leaves, Esteban lets loose his fury, throwing valuable statues and vases across the room, where they smash into pieces. Suddenly, Esteban stops and grabs the window frame. He gazes out into the hazy, humid night, watching the sunset colors light the evening sky. The bright orange, red, and purple, streak through the sky intermittently, behind the high-altitude cumulus clouds.

He slams his fists again, this time on the frame, and a simultaneous crack of thunder resounds across the camp. *I will* not *let this interfere with our plans ... We are too close.* His eyes scan the room, looking at the walls in search of inspiration and strength.

He locks his gaze onto the painting hanging on the wall across the room. He briskly makes his way to the far-side of the room, reaching out toward the portrait. Slowly raising his head, he looks up and then, deep in thought, runs his fingers over the oil painting of Jorge Valdez, the founder of RAFCO. The bumpy textures of the brush strokes are somehow soothing to Esteban, as if he can feel Jorge's energy. It has a calming effect and seems to help lessen his anger.

Reaper Two-Six
Year 6

I can't believe he's been gone more than six years.

Esteban recalls the day he took over as the leader of RAFCO, the day Jorge took ill and lay dying in his home. "Make me proud, Esteban," he'd said in a frail and shaky voice, mere hours before his death. "Continue my work."

Esteban looks at the painting and responds to that long-ago request, "I have brought our dream close to fruition Jorge. Soon you will look down and see how the world stands in awe of our brilliance, and fears our power."

Esteban returns to his desk, and calls Pancho, "Get the Aurora to the underground hanger. I want her ready by first light."

"But sir," Pancho says, "the aircraft isn't going to …"

"Don't give me excuses, Pancho, give me results. Or I will find another mechanic who can. I want her ready by morning, and I want you to be sure the runway is clear in case we need to launch her from the tunnel."

Knowing that, along with finding another mechanic, Esteban will find a deep hole to bury him in, Pancho has no choice but to bow down. "Yes sir, no problem sir," Pancho says, before Esteban breaks the call connection.

"Fucking wrench monkey," Esteban snaps at the phone. "You would think I'd asked him to paint the Mona Lisa. Snap two missiles into place and tell the navigation

computer to download the targeting info, that's all ...
Fucking piece of shit."

He dials Fernando's number and waits impatiently as
the phone rings once, twice.

Fernando answers with more than a little trepidation
in his voice, "Yes sir."

"I want you to get the J-20s into the air to patrol and
make sure the radar is fully manned. Everyone else ... Get
the vehicles packed and ready to bug out by 0900."

Esteban grabs a fine bottle of vintage Don Pilar Anejo
Tequila and adds, "When you are done, I want you to be sure
everyone sees the Aurora take flight in the morning." Lightly
shaking the Tequila bottle, he adds, "Tomorrow night in
Dibulla, we will celebrate the beginning of RAFCO's new
world."

After a few final words, Esteban ends the call.

Over twenty-five years ago, the area in and around
the camp was very desirable land, home to many affluent
Colombian statesmen. To provide transportation for
commerce and boost the local economy, many building
projects were undertaken; among them was the construction
of an extensive highway system.

Because of the terrain, tunnels capable of supporting
four-lane roadways were needed. Cut into the sides of dozens

of mountains, a few of the burrowed out tunnels are more than a mile long, slicing through the dense Colombian rock.

Over the years, as the drug cartels inched closer and closer to the area, the wealthy began moving away, while legitimate businesses relocated. The rugged land is extremely difficult to farm, so the towns were essentially abandoned once all the businesses left, and the jobs disappeared.

The RAFCO camp took over part of an abandoned town. The seventy-seven hundred-foot long tunnel on the far northeastern side was a nice bonus, although it wasn't looked upon as having much value until recently. After the surprise attack by the Reapers last year, Esteban decided to increase their ability to launch a retaliatory strike. He essentially created an underground hanger and runway system inside the tunnel, giving RAFCO a usable runway length of eleven thousand, five hundred feet. The old highway continues for another thirty-eight hundred feet beyond the backside of the mountain tunnel. The steep four thousand-foot mountains at the end of the thirty-eight hundred-foot section, is the only reason this runway isn't used. It would be a very difficult landing on that approach.

With the plan set, Esteban heads down to accompany the Aurora, leaving Fernando to coordinate all the remaining activities, including preparing the camp for the morning's departure and hunting down the escaped Americans.

Partially up the steep, wooded mountain, Doc grabs Professor's shoulder and says, "Hear that?" She points southwest toward RAFCO's main runway.

Professor slowly turns his head, at the same time a rumble of thunder rolls through the sky, and looks toward the horizon, following Doc's finger. To one side, dark clouds roll in; on the other side, the glare of the setting sun forces him to squint.

After a few seconds, the camp comes into focus and he thinks, *Shit ... We're not very far away yet.*

"Yea, I know," he says. "We're still too damn close, and we're going to get soaked. These woods are a total bitch, but at least they'll provide good cover."

"No, not the thunder," Doc snorts back.

Now, standing side-by-side, they listen intently, trying to reflect on what might be happening at this hour of the day in the RAFCO camp. It's usually pretty quiet around the evening meal.

A muffled, rumbling noise begins to fill the air around the Reapers that sounds man-made ... definitely not thunder. Due to the shape of the camp and the heavily wooded mountainous area, pinpointing the location of sounds is difficult.

After a few moments, they turn to face each other. Their faces clearly express the frustration and inability to pinpoint and identify the man-made sounds they hear. Unable to distinguish the noise, they decide to keep moving, believing distance is their friend, especially after sending the files to PVL.

Five minutes later, three J-20s streak into the sky. They turn and bank hard, passing close over the Reaper's location. Both Doc and Professor instinctually hit the ground, although the tree canopies nearly blanket the entire area.

As the sound of the J-20's engines begin to fade, Doc says, "Shit. I wasn't expecting they'd come after us with jets."

"I don't think those are for us," Professor says. "I got a quick glimpse, and they looked like the J-20s we encountered last year."

"Seriously?" she asks, her brow furrowed.

"I know. Doesn't make sense to me either," he says. "At least, we should be safe. Those 20s don't have thermal or infrared cameras. It would be next to impossible for them to spot us in this dense foliage without it."

"Then what the hell is going on?" Doc asks.

Reaper Two-Six
Year 6

After looking around, she points down the mountain at a small clearing and says, "Let's go have a look."

Reaching down into her pants pocket, Doc hands him a small pair of binoculars that she stole a few weeks after coming to the camp. She hid them successfully for months in their "suite" inside Professor's mattress.

"I was hoping you remembered to bring those," Professor says in an approving voice. "Okay. Let's go have a look."

The beautiful evening sky has now given way to the darkness of night, and the clouds suddenly give way to rain. As the drops fall harder, the Reapers navigate the undergrowth with only minimal and intermittent light from the crescent moon that occasionally breaks from behind the cloud cover.

"Fuck!" Professor suddenly exclaims, collapsing to the ground.

He grabs his left ankle as pulses of electrified pain shoot up the back of his leg and explode up his back.

Doc rushes to him, "What happened?"

"I must have stepped on some wet moss. My foot slipped right out from under me," he says, gritting his teeth. "Shit, I don't think it's broken, but, damn, it hurts."

Doc gets him to lay flat on his back and carefully examines his ankle. Clenching his teeth while she slowly rotates his ankle, she feels for any obvious fractures.

"I think it's just a sprain," Doc says, "but a bad one. It's already swelling." She's relieved that Professor's ankle isn't broken; but she's still anxious, her mind focused on the unusual activity radiating from the northern part of the camp — the Aurora's hanger.

Professor hands her back the binoculars and says, "Go on ahead. I'll catch up."

She nods reluctantly and continues down the mountain to the clearing, three hundred yards away.

Reaching the edge of the clearing, she squats down low to the ground and slithers into the tall grass. Pulling the binoculars out of her pocket, she scans the camp, quickly zeroing in on the northeast side, where the most activity appears to take place.

Fat raindrops splatter on the lenses, making it difficult to see, but one thing is certain, the large aircraft she can see through the binoculars is one she recognizes.

What the hell ... that's the Aurora! Where are they taking her?

As the aircraft is towed across the main runway, Doc watches intently. Due to poor lighting, the now steady rain, and the distance, she can see only indistinguishable shadows moving around near the plane.

Hmmm, ten… fifteen… twenty… twenty-two RAFCO associates around the Aurora. I wonder why there are so many people.

Her eyes are glued to the rain soaked and dripping binoculars. She watches as the Aurora continues to get closer and closer to some sort of building; a building very close to the side of the mountain … *Almost attached,* she thinks.

Two large doors on the building suddenly begin to slide apart. She stares silently as the Aurora slips inside the bowels of the mountain. She furrows her brow in confusion and worry.

What the hell is that place? A secret maintenance facility? A hardened bunker of some kind? How far back into the mountain does it go? Why are they hiding it now, after more than two weeks in the open hanger? Where are the missiles?

She slowly moves the binoculars from the mountainous hanger to the original hanger and back again, desperately looking for the missiles. *Nah,* she thinks. *They couldn't have attached them that quickly to the underbelly racks. Could they? Professor said twelve to eighteen hours before they'd be ready; ample time for PVL to get our FTP info to the Pentagon and then drop in a covert team of Seals*

here ... to stop this insanity.

She feels panic build as she thinks, *Are they getting*

ready to launch the Aurora? Now? So soon? In this weather?

She takes her eyes away from the binoculars for just a

few seconds, to look back up the mountain, hoping Professor

was making his way down. Not seeing any signs of him, she

returns to watching the Aurora. She sees the bay doors begin

to close and suddenly the lights come on within the hanger.

For a brief instant, the intensity of the light is too bright for

her eyes; she has to look away. Quickly returning to the

doors, she squints, trying to focus on as many details as she

can; burning the images into her mind.

About a minute later, the doors close tightly,

returning the northern side of the compound to darkness once

more. She moves her attention to the center of camp, but her

line of sight is poor, and she can't see much of anything. A

few portable lights dance around, but no definitive pattern of

activity registers from her vantage point.

Her thoughts drift to the inside of the mountain

hanger and what she saw just before the doors closed ... *a*

deep lighted tunnel. It almost looked like the top of an

aircraft carrier; long, narrow and pretty straight. Awfully

big for a simple underground storage facility.

Reaper Two-Six
Year 6

Suddenly, it hits her. She unconsciously mutters, "Shit!" She recalls the intel she'd gathered on this area of Colombia before she and Professor embarked on this mission. She had forgotten all about the abandoned tunnels, figuring they had nothing to do with their undercover mission. That was until now, when she saw the Aurora disappear into one.

Realizing she's collected all the information she can for the moment, she decides to head back up to Professor. Her concern now is that he won't be able to walk.

Crawling backward out of the tall grass, she stands up then carefully begins her trek back up the wooded mountain. She slips once, on the same thing that made Professor lose his footing — wet moss. Luckily, she grabs hold of a small tree and avoids a disaster. They can't afford for both of them to be injured.

About sixty yards up, she sees him. Obviously still in severe pain, he's managing to walk slowly on his ankle; hobbling and grabbing onto low-hanging branches to keep his balance. When she reaches him, they sit down behind a large tree.

Professor has tightly wrapped his bandana around his ankle to support it. *He's always been a fighter,* she muses. *A royal pain in the ass, but a good survivalist.*

Using a lot of animated hand gestures, an emotional and worried Doc begins to explain what she witnessed: the relocation of the Aurora.

For the next several minutes, he focuses on her every word. The sense of dread and urgency, and the feeling that they need to do more is nearly overwhelming.

A secret hanger and underground airstrip, Fuck! This just gets better and better, he ponders, *but what can we do?*

Doc insists that they need to investigate the underground hanger because it could seriously impact the success of any Seal team mission. No one has any clue that RAFCO has access to a secret tunnel. It never came up in any GDO briefing.

While Professor shares Doc's concern, he is equally worried about … At that moment, the J-20s buzz the camp again. The Reapers gaze skyward, watching the aircraft complete a 180-degree turn, to head back toward the coast.

"I think they're patrolling," Professor says. The fact that RAFCO has launched an air patrol is a signal to him that something is going to happen, and very soon.

Turning his eyes toward Doc, he says, "You're right. We need to investigate this. Let's get down to that secret hanger."

Chapter 17
The Incision

"Aw … Shit," Professor says, grinding his teeth in excruciating pain.

He collapses to the ground and slides backward, on his backside, settling into the brush against the side of the secret hanger building. He reaches down and unties the bandana, relieving some of the pain searing from his left ankle. The swelling has significantly grown over the past five hours, sending wave after wave of throbbing pain rocketing up his left leg. Sweat has soaked through his shirt. Now, because the rain cooled the temperature into the low sixties, he is shivering and grateful that daybreak will be soon.

Thank God, we made it, he thinks.

The long journey to the hanger caused him to favor his right foot for balance and walking. Now, his hip feels out of alignment; firing screaming nerve pulses up his back.

He looks up and notices the crisp, early morning blue-tinted rays of light starting to seep across the sky. The rain is softer now, barely sprinkling, although the sky is still mostly cloudy.

Fuck is the first word to come to mind. *It took much longer than it should have to get to the hanger, and it's my fault. Twisting my damned ankle is the last thing we needed. Shit ...shit ... shit.*

Doc feels Professor grab her shirt, pulling it; the look in his eyes pleads with her to sit down. She squats next to him and scans the area for RAFCO associates. With her senses heightened, she listens for even the slightest noise that feels out-of-place. It's clear, from his panting, sweating, and severe look of pain plastered all over his face that Professor is not going to make it much further.

She nods at him and thinks, *At least we made it here, to the hanger. I guess the rest is up to me.*

A moment later, she winces and looks skyward. *I wish those damn jets would quit buzzing overhead; it's really nerve-wracking.*

She snaps her head to the left, hearing a door click closed. Both Reapers hunker down low, and Professor pulls his knife; gripping it tightly in his sweaty palm.

A few seconds later, voices resonate from around the corner. Prostrating herself flat on the ground, she crawls to the edge of the hanger building. She can feel her stomach clench with increasing tension. Peering around the corner, she notes three men enjoying a smoke during the break in the rain.

I need to get in there to see what in the hell is going on, she reasons. *I'd rather avoid any unpleasantry, if possible.*

Her eyes scan the nearby area, when an idea pops into her head. She inches backward, signals Professor to stay put, then dashes into the woods. A few seconds later, she returns with a thick stick in her hand. Crawling back to the front of the building, she waits patiently.

She watches the soft orange glows of the RAFCO associate's cigarettes get closer to their faces. The billowing cloud of exhaled burned tobacco flows in her direction, slowly rising into the sky. The haziness of the cloud makes everything appear fuzzy and slightly distorted.

The three men, realizing they've been away from their posts long enough, took one final puff, and then flick their still lit cigarette butts into the air and head inside the hanger. As soon as the last associate crosses the door jam, Doc hustles her way to the opening; slipping the stick in between the frame and the door, preventing it from completely closing.

Sliding on her knees, she stops mere inches from the door. After listening against the wall, she decides to sneak inside.

Reaper Two-Six
Year 6

Grabbing the stick, she quietly eases the door open, praying it won't squeak or make a sound. The bright interior lights illuminate her, sending shivers of anxiety pumping through her veins.

Careful ... careful ... she repeats in her mind. *You don't want another panic attack. Take a few deep breaths.*

Spotting a path, she slips inside and, like a flash, dashes across the room, coming to rest behind a Jeep. Breathing deeply, Doc notices the distinctive musty smell within the tunnel.

How can they stand it? she thinks, moving her bandana over her nose and mouth, while the intensity of the smell nearly causes her to gag.

After taking in her surroundings, she whispers, "Oh my God. It really is an underground hanger."

As she looks at the clean and straight line of the surface the aircraft sits on, she exclaims under her breath once more, "Holy shit! It's a runway tunnel."

For the first few hundred feet of the tunnel, light fixtures are secured partway up the block-lined side walls. The glowing white light stretches down the runway portion of the tunnel, barely illuminating the mile-plus long section above a ghostly black. A speck of remaining moonlight sparkles at the far end, highlighting the opening on the backside of the mountain.

Doc inches her way around the Jeep, carefully peeking out from behind the corners and over its roof. Crates, stacks of supplies, weapons, and makeshift shelving are scattered along the tunnel walls. Neatly centered within the tunnel, the Aurora attracts the largest crowd of RAFCO associates.

A large wedge-shaped metallic structure anchored into the floor sits directly behind the aircraft. *An engine blast shield,* Doc thinks. *It looks as if it is hydraulically operated and able to recess into the floor, appearing to open and close similar to those on modern day aircraft carriers.* She shakes her head in disbelief. *This is a serious hidden operation.*

A layer of what looks like green moss covers a large portion of the tunnel's tall jagged rock ceiling. Noticeable wet spots sprinkle both walls, and standing water is present at various locations on the floor.

She decides to stay put as long as possible and simply listen. The acoustics in the hanger seem to carry voices a long way, and she can clearly understand numerous conversations.

For the next ten minutes, she focuses all her energy on listening and remembering, even though what she hears is raising her anxiety level exponentially.

"They can't be ... they just can't be," she keeps repeating in a whisper voice.

Without warning, a large whistle resonates throughout the hanger, followed by dozens of footsteps shuffling, then coming to a sudden stop. Doc's heart pounds, her head aches with worry, and her body tenses when she hears a strong, familiar voice begin to speak.

I think that's Esteban, she ponders.

A few minutes into his speech, Doc has heard enough.

Shit, is all she can think. *What are we going to do? They're planning to take off. We've got to stop them. We can't let them fly the Aurora on this mission of terror.*

Almost in a panic, she scurries out the door, slowing just enough to make sure the stick keeps the door partially open.

Plopping down next to Professor, her heart now pounding fiercely, she starts frantically explaining to Professor that RAFCO is getting ready to launch the Aurora. She tries to keep her voice low but it is difficult considering the urgency of what she has just learned. She continues to share the details of what she heard, and also the layout inside the hanger, around the Aurora and down the runway tunnel.

He firmly grips her shoulders and stares into her eyes. He has an idea, but needs to know a few very specific things to see if she can be trusted to pull it off before suggesting it. As he speaks, she focuses on his every word.

Doc returns Professor's steady gaze and answers his questions.

Seeing her composure has returned, Professor begins to explain his idea. She nods in understanding and acknowledgement as he lays out his plan.

With no time for a serious debate, they agree and bump knuckles, as if to say, *Let's do it.*

Professor hands her the knife, grabs his bandana, and stuffs it into his mouth. Doc rolls up his sleeve to the shoulder, locating the temporary tattoo. She swallows hard and makes an incision right in the center of the tattoo.

Professor's muffled scream startles her at first, causing her hand to shake and stop cutting into his flesh. The blood begins to flow from the wound; it runs down the outside of his arm and drips onto the moist, black soil. She looks at him with hesitation in her eyes. He grits his teeth harder, clenches his fists, looks up at her, and nods several times, almost frantic in his mind for her to continue.

She proceeds to cut deep into his arm, carefully separating layer after layer of muscle fiber, connective tissue and skin cells. The blood, now pouring from the incision, collects in a dark, sticky pool on the ground. Professor's arm begins to shake and he writhes in pain. Doc is nearly sick to her stomach listening to him spew muted obscenities. His brow is now full of sweat running down the sides of his face and into his eyes as he desperately tries to focus on anything but the pain sizzling up his shoulder and roaring across his back.

Starting to have difficulty seeing into her cut, Doc blows on the open wound, trying to displace the blood enough to continue digging deeper. A new massive river of pain blasts into Professor's body. Doc can see he is beginning to show symptoms of passing out.

With a few final, tremendously quick deep cuts, she finally pulls out the item she seeks, the buried treasure — a wet and glistening with blood, Reaper GPS homing beacon.

"Got it," she says with relief.

In a response of his own, Professor collapses near her feet, from exhaustion.

She takes the bandana out of his mouth and tightly wraps it around the cut on his arm as a tourniquet. Doc then dashes for the door once more.

Professor rolls over onto his back and catches heaving breaths as the ravages of the recent surgery roll through his body. He will rest for a short while — but only a very short while — until he needs to get back into action.

Doc takes a quick look inside the hanger. Seeing the path is clear, she sprints across the room, coming to rest behind the Jeep again. Glancing around the vehicle's front tires, she spots an opportunity and bolts for the side wall, snaking behind stacks of tires and a large stand containing a partially damaged engine.

Hmmm, she thinks. *I wonder if we did that last year.* A smirk makes its way onto her face. *When I get back to the GDO, I need to remember to tell Viral that I've seen his squadron's work;* if *I get back, and* if *there is something to go back to ...* Shaking off the negative thoughts, she waits patiently.

Outside the hanger, Professor finally makes it to his feet, still a little woozy from blood loss and physical exhaustion that the strong pain caused.

"I don't know which hurts worse now: my ankle or my arm," he mutters. "I'm going to need a vacation after this shit, and not three days in a soaking wet Bangkok this time. No, I want three fucking weeks on the beach in Naxos, Greece. No cell phones, no computers, nothing except peaceful sunshine and alcohol." He chuckles quietly. He almost forgets his pain for a second, but reality comes slamming back.

He trudges painfully to the front edge of the secret hanger building and looks around. *All clear, let's do this. May God be with you, Doc.*

Professor stumbles his way across the edge of the runway and hops into a Hummer. After a quick glance around the front seat, he finds the keys and turns the ignition ON. The deep throated, guttural engine growls to life. *Oh, niiiiicccce,* he thinks.

He moves the Hummer into position and blasts the horn for five seconds. He waits a few moments and then blasts it again for five seconds. He keeps repeating this until …

Yes, he grins as the hanger doors start to open. *That stick did the trick, keeping them from exiting the building to investigate so they had to open the main hanger door.*

Now, he continuously blasts the horn, trying to get as many RAFCO associates out into the open as he can. He watches over his shoulder with his foot on the accelerator, ready to jam the pedal to the floor. As the associates get close to the Hummer, he'll punch it and race down the runway, running down anyone that gets in his way. Once at the far end, he'll ram through the front gate, finally gone ... *gone* ... for good from this God forsaken place.

Inside the secret hanger, Doc watches Esteban yell at the two pilots in the Aurora's cockpit. He then swings his hand in the air and points straight down the tunnel. *No!* she thinks. *Not yet.*

The cockpit canopy starts to close while Esteban turns and heads for the hanger door. Without worry or concern for her own safety, she launches herself out into the open and darts under the Aurora's left wing. Reaching out, she grabs the landing gear strut to stop her forward motion, whacking her chest against the tires.

"Oof!" She nearly doubles over in pain.

The subsonic jet engines begin to spool-up, emitting their familiar high pitched piercing whine, followed by the whoosh of the engines igniting. Within seconds, the engines begin swallowing enormous amounts of air as the RAFCO pilots push the throttles forward, preparing for takeoff.

Doc wraps both her hands around the landing gear main strut and pulls herself up onto the gear assembly. Wrapping her legs around the landing gear mechanism to ensure she doesn't get sucked into the engine intakes, she reaches down into the bottom of her left pants pocket.

Tightly grasping Professor's homing beacon between three fingers, she begins to pull her hand out of her pocket.

At that moment, the engines accelerate to full power, sending vibrational waves buzzing throughout the entire aircraft. The Aurora lurches forward, causing Doc to grab hold with both arms; the beacon still tightly grasped in her hand.

Realizing she has only seconds left, she looks up and finds a protected location. With a swift crisp motion, she reaches inside the landing gear bay and securely wedges Professor's GPS beacon into a tight spot.

"This better work," she says.

She and Professor are putting their ultimate hope on the fact that the beacon will automatically begin transmitting its location when exposed to temperatures below sixty degrees Fahrenheit (sixteen degrees Centigrade). As far as they know, sixty degrees is the threshold for the device. The original intention was to be able to locate and recover a dead body. Their hope is that the GPS beacon will activate when the Aurora climbs above five thousand feet, depending upon the exact atmospheric conditions.

Travelling at more than forty knots, Doc releases her tight grip and executes a perfect rolling dismount from the landing gear. After lying flat on the ground to wait for the remainder of the aircraft to zip past overhead, she finally dodges for the side of the tunnel runway, taking refuge in an abandoned maintenance doorway. She crouches, still keeping an eye on the Aurora. The exhaust flames intensify as the aircraft gains speed near the end of the tunnel.

Within seconds, the aircraft pops out of the tunnel opening and into the morning sunrise. A few moments later, the Aurora lifts off, vanishing from her view, leaving behind only the thunderous rumbling reverberation off the walls.

Her heart suddenly sinks. *I guess we'll know in an hour or two if PVL gets the beacon and is successful in taking these bastards down.* Then, with tightness in her stomach, a thought begins to envelope her, like a child's nightmare, and a devastating thought flashes through her mind, *What if we fail?*

Reaper Two-Six
Year 6

Chapter 18
It Must Be Done
Carnarvon, Western Australia

Still rummaging through hours and hours of X-47 drone video at the Australian GDO command center, Wolverine has been awake for thirty-eight straight hours. His fingertips have started to shake because of the large amount of caffeine he's consumed.

Suddenly, Red Diamond bursts through his door, "I got him! I got him! I got a lock on Professor's beacon!" he announces from the doorway. His face is flushed with excitement.

Wolverine spins his chair around, leaps to his feet, and runs with Red Diamond around the corner and down the narrow hallway. He enters the main command center room and asks, "Where is he?"

"He appears to be in an aircraft traveling north from western Colombia. The aircraft is gaining speed and altitude rapidly," Red Diamond says. "He's passing through twenty thousand feet and is showing no signs of leveling off."

"Send Professor's signal to the large screen and overlay it on the global map. Do you have Doc yet?"

Red Diamond punches a few keystrokes. A glowing green dot appears on the wall-mounted LCD big screen. Wolverine moves forward, touches the screen with two fingers, and slowly moves them apart; the world map zooms in. He repeats the zooming process until he has just the Caribbean Sea, with the surrounding land masses from the Americas on the screen.

"No sir. Negative on Doc's signal," Red Diamond says, shaking his head. He shrugs and gives the Admiral a puzzled look. *What the hell,* he thinks. *Even if she's dead, we should still be able to ping her. It just doesn't make sense.*

"Pipe this through the network to PVL. Do whatever you have to do with the server traffic. This has priority number one." Wolverine tells Red Diamond.

"Yes sir."

Wolverine monitors the altitude, speed and directional information of the unknown aircraft containing Professor's homing beacon. As he watches, he formulates a plan to obtain more intel on the situation.

He looks over at Fox's screen and points at the objects moving over the RAFCO camp, "Fox, are those J-20s still patrolling the RAFCO HQ?"

The long-range visual cameras on the X-47 spotted the aircraft circling the RAFCO camp, and the Reapers were able to identify them before getting spotted themselves.

"Yes sir. They've been there all night."

"Damn. We need to get closer. Just a few clear images might shed some light on the situation," Wolverine says while pacing the room deep in thought. His eyes move from screen to screen, collecting and assimilating situational awareness data: weather, video, satellite imagery, current aircraft status, etc.

Pausing for a moment, he has an idea. Walking over to the main landline phone, he picks up the headset and taps in a few numbers. Several seconds later, the call is answered. His voice is polite as he says, "This is Fleet Admiral Wolverine from the GDO. Please get me Captain Shaw."

The USS Carl Vinson, under the command of Captain Alan Shaw, is sailing in the eastern Pacific Ocean, currently west of Costa Rica. Captain Shaw is on deck, watching the latest drills. He hears his name over the PA system and heads to the bridge to take the call.

"Wolverine, it's good to hear your voice," he says. "Your boys arrived several hours ago and are settling in nicely. How's Australia treating you?"

Ignoring the social chit-chat, Wolverine cuts right to the reason for his call. "Captain, we've got a situation. We're currently tracking an aircraft heading out of Colombia, and I'm not sure of its intentions. I need my X-47s to get some good shots of the RAFCO camp, but it's being patrolled. Would you be willing to send some of your boys, along with Captain Viral's squadron, to run them off?"

"How many fighters are we talking here, Wolverine?"

"Three that we know of in the air, and more may be on the ground."

"Do you think they'll put up a fight?"

"Probably."

"I need to get approval then. I can't allow my guys to get fired upon unless we have clearance to defend ourselves. Plus, we'll be in Colombian airspace without approval, so the State Department must be notified."

Wolverine takes his ear away from the phone and is about ready to smash it on the desk. *This is exactly why the GDO was formed,* he thinks. *We had preapproval to go after terrorists in all supporting countries. Good Lord. The U.S. is so tied up in red tape.*

Regaining his composure, he realizes it's not Captain Shaw's fault. Returning the phone to the side of his face, Wolverine says. "Do what you must Captain, but please get my boy's launched as quick as possible. I need intel within the hour."

"Will do."

They hang up. Wolverine's eyes drift across the room; he squints, looking at the numbers on the screen. Getting up slowly, he walks toward the large LCD display, intensely gazing at the continually updating information on Professor's beacon. The growing tension ache from his neck begins to flow up the back of his head.

What in the hell? As Wolverine looks at the data, something clicks.

He quickly turns to Red Diamond and asks, "Is this right?" He points to the GPS readout data on the screen.

"Yes sir."

What's he in? Wolverine ponders.

Suddenly, realizing the speed and altitude match only one aircraft — the Aurora — he begins to anxiously wonder. *That can't be. Without Doc? Something's not right.*

Wolverine continues to stare at the rapidly changing beacon information; the green dot has already moved off the Colombian coast and is nearly halfway to Cuba. It's accelerating toward … *The Florida coast?* he thinks. *Why? What's Professor thinking?*

Wolverine's instincts begin to set off internal alarms. During his younger years, he was reserved about trusting his feelings. As his military responsibilities grew, he learned how to control and understand those feelings; even trust them.

"Red Diamond, give me a minute-by-minute projected path of the aircraft for the next sixty minutes," Wolverine barks. "Assume current speed and directional information."

A dotted line appears on the screen, originating from the middle of the Caribbean Sea, finally ending over northeastern Virginia.

"Damn. What's going on, Professor?" Wolverine mutters.

His eyes dart around the room while he thinks, hoping the data will expose Professor's real intentions. *Talk to me, my friend. You know better than to fly an unknown aircraft that close to the U.S. capital.*

Wolverine sits down and continues to watch the aircraft's actual flight path, comparing it to the projected one. *Shit,* is all he can think.

All types of scenarios race through his mind. *Why is Professor taking that particular flight path? None of this makes any sense.*

Shaking his head, Wolverine is forced to make a difficult conclusion; Professor must be in the aircraft unwillingly, maybe even as a hostage. *I hope I'm wrong, but you're definitely in the Aurora,* he thinks. *Why? And where's Doc?*

Wolverine takes a few moments to gather his thoughts, and then makes a necessary painful decision. *I don't have a choice,* he thinks. *I have a responsibility to report all suspicious activity that might endanger lives. Sorry, Professor. I sure hope you make your intentions known before it's too late.*

He grabs his cell phone and punches a few buttons. Seconds later, a pleasant voice says, "Hello."

"Hi, Julie, it's Wolverine. Is Secretary Mallory available?"

"I'm sorry, sir." Julie says. "He's on a flight to Las Vegas to meet with Secretary Dow at Nellis AFB. He'll be landing in two hours. Can I have him call you then?"

This will all be over in two hours, he thinks.

"Yes please," is all he manages to say, lost in thought about his next step. *There is no way the Reapers can get to that aircraft in time; I need the Air Force or Navy to intercept it, and fast.*

Reaper Two-Six
Year 6

Scanning his mind for the next name, he finally says, "Any chance you can you ring Secretary Dow for me? I don't have the number at his current assignment."

"Absolutely, sir. Just a moment, I'll patch you through."

The passing of every second pounds tension and anxiety throughout Wolverine's entire being. His left eye is starting to twitch as his stress level climbs.

The aircraft's trajectory is etched into his brain, like a hot searing knife, the intensity and gravity of the situation burns deep within him. The thought of launching a strike against Professor sickens him. *It sure looks like he's giving me no choice,* he thinks.

"Go ahead, Admiral Wolverine," Julie says. "Do you need anything else, sir?"

"Thanks Julie. I'm all set. I appreciate your help."

"Good day, gentlemen," she says, and disconnects from the call.

"Wolverine, did you find our bird yet?" Secretary Dow says. The smugness in his voice makes Wolverine want to jump through the phone and wring his scrawny neck.

"Actually, Mr. Secretary, I believe we have," Wolverine says. He's hesitant to announce the situation as a fact because Professor's life weighs heavily on his mind.

"Where?" Secretary Dow asks.

"Sir, that's the issue. I'm tracking something right now that is traveling at a speed and altitude consistent with the Aurora. But," Wolverine swallows and clears his throat, horrified by what he's about to say. "It appears to be on a course for the DC area."

"Where is it *right* now?" Secretary Dow demands.

"Passing just west of Jamaica and continuing northward."

A flurry of activity breaks out in Secretary Dow's temporary office in the Area 51 HQ building. All Wolverine can hear is paper shuffling and a muffle of voices.

Suddenly, Secretary Dow says, "Hang on, Wolverine. I'm going to get some F-22s scrambled out of Tyndall Air Force Base. We'll give them the coordinates shortly, but I want them airborne right away. I'm going to put Langley on alert, too."

After a few seconds, he continues, "Can the Aurora's radar pick up the 22s?"

"Doubtful," Wolverine replies.

"Good. That'll buy us some time as they can get close, before we decide what to do."

"Mr. Secretary?" Wolverine asks. He gets no reply. "Sir?"

Reaper Two-Six
Year 6

Secretary Dow has put down the phone and is now speaking with both Air Force base commanders.

Wolverine glances over his shoulder and sees seven blue dots appear on the screen, near the northern tip of South America.

Viral's Storm Reapers, he concludes. *Good. Maybe that'll be enough to clear the patrol so I can get some shots of RAFCO's camp. At least this time, we've got the surprise advantage*, he thinks, recalling how the attack ended last year.

Wolverine taps his foot faster and faster the more time passes without definitive data. He knows they can't just follow the Aurora, as it will outrun anything they have. The fighters will have to approach from the front or partial side of the Aurora's projected flight path and have only one chance to act.

The thought continues to churn his stomach as he thinks, *Professor ... Professor ... Professor ... What* are *you doing?* Then, he almost dry heaves with the anxiety he's feeling. *I won't lose another,* remembering what happened to Elena. He blamed himself for her death, and it was almost the end of him, emotionally. *I can't lose another,* he thinks repeatedly.

Reaper Two-Six
Year 6

"Send me the Aurora's tracking information. We'll take it from here," Secretary Dow says.

The silence begins to anger him. He raises his voice saying, "Wolverine?"

Still no response. Secretary Dow practically yells into the receiver, "Wolverine!"

Snapping his attention back to the situation, Wolverine snatches up the phone and says, "Sir … yes sir … sorry, sir."

Secretary Dow repeats his request, now with a more demanding edge in his voice. "Send me the Aurora's tracking information to this secure FTP site. We'll take it from here."

He gives Wolverine the details of the site over the phone. Wolverine quickly writes them down, gives them to Red Diamond, and hastily waves a hand signal letting him know it's urgent.

"Okay, sir, got it," Wolverine says to Secretary Dow. "I'll have the information sent to you immediately. If I may, the beacon we are tracking is from one of my Captains. He's been undercover for many months, and this is the first we've heard from him, well, sort of. All we have is this signal."

"Why the hell is he onboard the Aurora?" the Secretary barks.

"Unknown, sir, and that's my concern. He may be trying to return it." Wolverine's not sure he believes that, but he can't discount it either.

"By flying to the capital of the United States," Secretary Dow roars in disbelief. "If that's the case, your pilots are dumber than I thought. If I can't raise the Aurora on the comm, then it and whoever is flying it is going to end up at the bottom of the ocean!"

The Secretary's derogatory statements about his Reapers infuriate Wolverine. He flies out of his seat and stomps down the hallway, ready to rip a new asshole the size of Texas into this arrogant Secretary's hind end. Slamming the door to his study, he opens his mouth, ready to unleash the verbal beast, when suddenly he catches a glimpse of her photo: Brooke.

He clenches his jaw, grinding his teeth, closes his eyes, and slowly sits on the couch. The raging emotions within him start to subside as he remembers, *I am just one part of a global crime-fighting cog. We are on the same side of this war wheel, Secretary Dow and me.*

The war wheel can only turn and be useful with cooperation from all sides of the government. Wolverine knows that if he alienates or severely pisses off Secretary

Dow, he does more harm to the ultimate goal: reducing global terrorism.

The result would be one more nail in the GDO financial coffin if the President of the United States decides not to continue funding. Somehow, this whole mess has to turn out successfully ... somehow ...

Wolverine takes a few deep breaths, then offers Secretary Dow a polite reply. "I understand, sir. I have two X-47s ready to fly over the RAFCO HQ. I respectfully ask that you keep me in the loop, sir."

Secretary Dow reins in his emotions and empathizes with Wolverine's position; he'd probably feel the same about one of his men.

"I'll contact President Mason within the next ten minutes and brief him. If you'd like to be on the line, I'll allow. But, so help me, Wolverine, if you try ..."

"I completely understand, sir," Wolverine says. "You'll have my full cooperation. Thank you, sir."

After a long pause and an unconscious nod, indicating, *he agrees*, Secretary Dow says, "Alight. I'll have Julie tie you in. Does she have your contact information?"

"She does."

"Here's my cell phone number, 555-498-7472. If you obtain any new intel, contact me immediately," the Secretary says.

The two men say their goodbyes, and then end the call. Wolverine snaps his cell phone shut and drops it on the pillow beside him.

He bends his head down toward his knees and places his hands over his face mumbling, "Dear God. What now?"

Chapter 19
The Fragmented Mirage
Over the Caribbean

The Aurora zooms through the sky at Mach 5.2 and seventy-five thousand feet. Currently passing over Cuba, the remainder of the aircraft's planned flight takes it west of the Bahamas, then north, toward the Carolina coast. Finally, journeying inland near Wilmington, the Aurora is now less than twenty-four minutes from simultaneous missile launch.

The payload is two Russian built 350-kiloton nuclear tipped missiles, tightly packed inside the Aurora's underbelly missile bay. The P-500 supersonic cruise missiles are modified for high altitude flight. Due to their immense size, the missiles are essentially stacked, one on top of the other, within the missile compartment. Once the pilot or the rear seat reconnaissance systems officer activates the launch button, the Aurora's outer bay doors will open. The missiles will then automatically release ten seconds apart, free-falling from the plane approximately two hundred feet before their rocket engine ignites.

Once lit, the missile's engine cannot be turned off. The guidance system will manipulate the missile's control surfaces in order to climb to 158,400 feet, then level off at the detonation altitude. The missile will rip through the sky at Mach 2.5, following its preprogrammed course, until it explodes over its target, showering the entire eastern United States in a massive EMP strike.

At Tyndall Air Force Base, twelve F-22s tear into the sky, two-by-two, their afterburners glowing in the familiar bright orange-pink diamond exhaust pattern. The thundering sound reverberates for miles around the Florida panhandle's coastal base.

Located east-southeast of Pensacola, Tyndall provides training for F-22 Raptor pilots. The facility also supports NORAD in their air dominance activities. As a front line resource, Tyndall receives the latest technology — from aircraft, to weapons, to maintenance techniques, everything needed to maintain the United States' air superiority.

The F-22s begin their climb to forty-four thousand feet and turn southward. The squadron commander, Lieutenant Colonel Jack Martin, verifies the uplink from Secretary Dow, and confirms the navigational system is locked onto the beacon's signal.

"Damn, that thing is really moving," Lieutenant Colonel Martin says. Checking his instruments and screens, he announces to the squadron, "Fifteen minutes to intercept, gentlemen. Set your missiles to data link targeting mode.

Reaper Two-Six
Year 6

This will ensure that the beacon's GPS data from your onboard computer will navigate the missile until the self-homing distance is reached."

After an affirming "roger" from all of his wingmen, Lieutenant Colonel Martin splits his squadron into north (Bravo) and south (Alpha) squadrons. Major George Sutherland will lead Bravo squadron, while Lieutenant Colonel Martin will continue with Alpha squadron.

The early morning sun penetrates the F-22's large monolithic polycarbonate canopy, gleaming off the top of the pilot's helmet. The dark tinted visor insulates the pilot's eyes from the intense glare, allowing him to maintain focus on the mission — preventing the unknown aircraft from inflicting damage on the United States.

At the designated coordinates, Lieutenant Colonel Martin says, "Bravo squadron, break. Good luck, Major."

He salutes in the cockpit as six Bravo squadron F-22s turn eastward. They will continue their course until they reach the Atlantic Ocean. The six Alpha squadron fighters continue southeastward, where they will engage the Aurora first.

Sitting in the GDO's main control room, Wolverine listens by speakerphone to the minute-by-minute discussion between President Mason, Secretary Dow, Lieutenant Colonel Martin, and Major Sutherland.

Prior to the F-22's departure, Wolverine took part in a conference call between Secretary Dow and President Mason. During that phone call, Wolverine listened helplessly to the details of the current mission. His stomach sank as he realized the dire circumstances that lay ahead for his friend and fellow Reaper, Professor.

Now, as the seconds tick away and the time of intercept nears, Wolverine shakes his head sadly, thinking, *Professor, Professor.*

Wolverine and all of his available staff furiously scan through dozens and dozens of images from satellites, stealth drones, previous recon missions, anything to try to clarify the situation with the Aurora. The Storm Reaper's squadron is still twenty minutes away from engaging the J-20's over the RAFCO HQ. Wolverine has also not heard anything from PVL for the past twenty-two hours. The staff tirelessly searches for a proverbial needle in the haystack.

Come on, Wolverine silently urges his staff; *find something, something ... anything at all.* He wants to know definitively whether Professor and Doc are on the aircraft that will soon be in the F-22's cross-hairs.

Reaper Two-Six
Year 6

Long-range ground-based cameras in southern Florida lock onto the GPS beacon's signal and identify the unknown aircraft as the Aurora by its shape and size. Space Shuttle and other NASA related missions have used this type of optical identification in the past. This is the first official confirmation Wolverine has heard that the aircraft has been identified.

As this is considered a national security threat, a high speed aircraft of unknown origin and unknown intention, the President has given authorization to shoot-down the Aurora if no communications have been established within the next five minutes.

Wolverine has heard enough and lowers the volume on the speaker phone, realizing he can do nothing now but wait and hope.

I need to focus on something useful, he thinks, still scanning through image after image on the screen in front of him. He sneaks a peek over his left shoulder to check on the status of the Storm Reapers. *Getting there ... I hope they run those J-20s out of Colombia for good.*

With the impressive stealth characteristics of the F-22s, Lieutenant Colonel Martin expects to sneak up undetected and come within a few miles of the Aurora before initiating the attack. And because the F-22s are almost five miles below the Aurora in altitude, the missiles will have a large vertical gap to close before locking on with their internal homing system.

The Aurora, currently traveling at almost a mile per second, is faster than the Mach 4 AIM-120C missiles carried by the F-22s in their concealed underbelly bays. This is why a front angled shot is necessary; positioning the Aurora to fly right into the missiles' path.

As the seconds tick away, Alpha squadron gets closer and closer to the Aurora. Lieutenant Colonel Martin is intensely focused on the navigational map.

Steady, steady, he repeats like a mantra ... *Almost there* ... now!

He flips the lever to open the missile bay doors and quickly scans the targeting computer screen. He verifies that the two missiles lock onto the Aurora's beacon.

"Stand by," Lieutenant Colonel Martin calls out over the comm system. "Ten seconds."

Watching the weapons systems computer tick down, he calls out, "Three... two ... one ... fox three!"

All six aircraft launch two missiles each. The sky erupts in fire and smoke as the missiles make an immediate and steep upward turn. The Aurora's flight path locks into each missile's brain. The large arcing exhaust contrails engulf the entire squadron in a grayish-white billowing cloud.

In the Aurora's rear seat, the officer spots numerous suspicious radar returns a few seconds before the missiles release. Once the F-22's bay doors open, their stealth characteristics are significantly degraded and can be picked up by sensitive radar systems, like those on the Aurora.

The Aurora's main defenses are stealth and speed. With the Aurora's stealth seemingly penetrated *somehow*, the pilot decides to try to outrun the missiles. Just before the missiles were launched, the Aurora pilot shoved the throttles full forward. Then, unlocking the safety device, he continues pushing the throttles until the emergency power activates. The engines swell and glow with incredible force, rapidly accelerating the Aurora. Both men's heads snap back against the rest while their bodies' compress into the seat by the increasing g-forces.

The pilot watches as the speed quickly increases — Mach 5.5 … Mach 6.2 … Mach 7.0 … Mach 7.2 — finally stabilizing at Mach 7.6, nearly four thousand knots!

"Holy shit!" Lieutenant Colonel Martin says. "I've never seen anything accelerate that fast. This is going to be close."

The twelve missiles from the F-22s blaze a trail, almost vertical now, as they race to intercept the Aurora. Less than a mile from their target, the onboard homing systems takes over navigation. The movable rear tail fins twist and turn in response to the course corrections calculated by the missiles' inertial autopilot. The smart proximity fusing detonation system becomes active, arming its forty-pound high-explosive blast-fragmentation warhead. The final autonomous terminal homing sequence begins.

With its wingtips starting to glow a glistening orange, infused with slight shades of red, the Aurora sears through the sky, nearly cutting it in half. The air is rippled by the vacuum created by the Aurora's fuselage slicing through the sky.

Without warning, the sky ruptures in a sea of devastating explosions. One after another, the twelve missiles' proximity fuses detonate, spewing thousands of hot high energy fragments. The accompanying blast shock waves pierce the air, sending bolts of energy radiating outward; thundering reverberations bounce off the F-22's cockpit canopies, resonating fiercely inside the pilot's helmet.

The painful ear ringing is quickly replaced by an outburst of celebratory cheers over the comm. President Mason, Secretary Dow, and even Wolverine slouch back into their chairs, believing the imminent threat is gone. Even a few of the Reapers listening closely to the teleconference exchange high-fives.

Wolverine's thoughts drift toward Doc and Professor. His eyes gloss over as he assumes he's never going to see them again. *The not knowing is worse than knowing,* he thinks. The only consolation is that the United States is safe.

He pulls himself out of the chair and stretches his back. For more than thirty minutes, he's been sitting hunched over his laptop, an extremely tense and uncomfortable position. Twisting his shoulders left and then right, he hears a couple of discs in his spine pop.

His eyes catch the main screen. A glowing green beacon is active and still moving northward. His heart jumps into his throat. He whips around, slaps the mute button to the off position and says, "It's still active. I repeat … the target is *still* active!"

Reaper Two-Six
Year 6

Chapter 20
Straight Shot
East of central Florida, United States

The Aurora's enormous speed and energy overshadowed the F-22's missiles. The destructive cloud of searing deadly particles exploded in the Aurora's wake; twenty yards behind its vertical stabilizers. For most encounters, this might be a kill shot. But this is not a normal situation, this is not a typical aircraft, this is the Aurora — the world's fastest and most advanced aircraft.

After the detonation of the F-22's missiles, the fragmented particles are flung outward in all directions, with high velocity. Unfortunately, the hull-piercing particles are no match for the Mach 7+ speed of the Aurora. Coming nowhere close to impacting the Aurora's skin, the remnants of the missiles begin their fourteen-mile journey to the ocean. A few unlucky migratory birds are all that the missiles' fragments might injure now.

The Aurora's cockpit is a bustling hive of activity. Neither the pilot nor the rear seat officer has any idea how they were being tracked. They've decided to move up their launch window as much as possible.

"We have to get close though, so the nukes don't miss their target," the Aurora's pilot tells his back seat officer.

The officer responds, "Yes sir. I already have it calculated. I'm ready to start the countdown."

"Do it," the pilot orders.

"Roger."

The rear seat officer flips a few switches and then, pressing one final button, he announces, "Done ... five minutes and counting."

The chatter on the teleconference amongst the President, Secretary Dow, Wolverine, and both squadron leaders is getting out of control, turning almost into a hysterical shout-fest. Becoming increasingly frustrated, Wolverine sits back in his chair, an exasperated look on his face, matched by the intense irritation he feels.

"Good Lord," he says in a whispered voice. "If they don't quit fucking around, they're going to lose this opportunity."

They just need a straight shot, he thinks. *The altitude difference between the Aurora and the F-22s must have hindered the missiles from obtaining a direct impact. Unfortunately, I don't think I have a voice in this mission. No one wants to listen to me.*

Reaper Two-Six
Year 6

It takes all his self-control to keep his mouth shut as he listens to Secretary Dow's mouth flapping like a flag in a storm. With his teeth gritted to prevent speaking out, Wolverine thinks, *Damn it Dow, shut the fuck up and let the pilots who happen to be closest to the action make the decision on what move to make now. Trust them to do their job.*

Wolverine is clearly on the President's side now. By executing an evasive maneuver and avoiding the twelve missiles, it's clear the Aurora has harmful intentions. What those intentions are is still unknown.

Part of Wolverine aches for the Aurora to survive because of Professor; but the rational part of him knows that they cannot afford to let the Aurora survive.

Focusing his attention back to the current shouting match spewing out of the phone, Wolverine's mind races *Christ … The Aurora knows about us now. We'll be damn lucky to get a second attempt with Bravo squadron. Every second these political assholes spend bickering …*

Wolverine suddenly locks onto an idea and quickly raises his hand, snapping his fingers twice, followed by a hand motion indicating, *come here.* Fox punches the autopilot button on his X-47 control panel, removes his headset, gets up and walks over to Wolverine.

Wolverine whispers instructions to Fox and hands him a key.

Fox dashes down the narrow hallway, returning only a few seconds later. He hands Wolverine an orange folder and returns the key.

"Thanks mate," Wolverine says to Fox.

Nodding, Fox returns to his flight control station.

Wolverine opens the folder and quickly thumbs through a few pages. Finding what he's looking for, he places a finger on the page, about three-quarters of the way down.

"Got it," he says with an energetic smile.

"Excuse me, Mr. President," Wolverine interrupts respectfully into the speakerphone.

The discussion continues as if he's said nothing. Realizing that he must get their attention, Wolverine takes a full breath and powerfully says in his deep voice, "Mr. President, sir, I know how we can shoot down the Aurora. Please sir, we're wasting precious time."

Like a knife popping a balloon, the air rushes out of the teleconference; it's now dead quiet.

"Admiral Wolverine, please continue," President Mason says, anxious to hear what he has to say.

Wolverine explains. "The first attack missed because the Aurora was able to escape the missiles' intercept course. It's simply too fast for a shot from below.

"We need to use the Aurora's extreme speed to our advantage, instead of fighting against it. At its current hypersonic velocity, the Aurora is not very maneuverable. Therefore, it's quite vulnerable to a direct frontal attack.

"I just pulled the classified documents from the F-22's testing, and I strongly recommend that Bravo squadron perform a full afterburner climb to maximum altitude. By the book, they can easily reach sixty-five thousand feet, but I'm betting the F-22s will make it well above seventy thousand feet. You know those engineers and their technical writing, conservative to the end.

"At that altitude, the F-22s will have an almost perfect straight-line shot to their target. The Aurora is probably anticipating another attack, but they'll never guess it to be from directly in front of them. The Aurora's pilots are most likely watching their belly more than anything else, figuring they can outrun any missile attack."

Wolverine sits back, a little more relaxed now that he's said his peace. *That's all I can do,* he thinks. *It's up to them now to decide.*

Reaper Two-Six
Year 6

The silence on the phone is worrisome to Wolverine. *Did I totally piss them off by interrupting like that? Are they too dense or too arrogant to listen to someone else's suggestions? Shit.*

A few low voices start to seep out of the speakerphone. A moment later, President Mason says, "Do it, Mr. Secretary ... now!"

"Yes sir." Secretary Dow says. "Major Sutherland, punch it. Knock that bastard out of the sky!"

As the Aurora rapidly streaks closer to Bravo squadron's location, all six F-22 pilots forcefully shove their throttles to maximum power and briskly pull back on their sticks. With the F-22's thrust-to-weight ratio greater than one, the aircraft look more like rockets, zipping skyward at an astounding rate.

"Forty-five seconds, boys," Major Sutherland says over the comm system. "Our bogie's coming straight at us red hot. Stand by to open the doors. Computers are locked on target."

"Come on, baby, come on," Major Sutherland says. His eyes focus with intensity on the altimeter and the beacon's signal.

As the F-22s slowly cross the seventy-two thousand-foot threshold, their rate of climb has fallen to under a thousand feet per minute. Major Sutherland presses his lips together in a grim line, not believing they'll make it to seventy-five thousand feet before the Aurora passes by them. Keeping his eyes pinned to the altimeter, he shakes his head slightly and orders the attack.

"Open the outer bay doors … *now!*"

"Three … two … one … fox three!" Major Sutherland says to his squadron over the comm system.

Twelve missiles roar to life, showering the F-22s with streams of white billowy smoke. The missiles' exhaust flames extend more than twenty-five feet behind their tail fins. With the missiles accelerating to Mach 4, the encounter will be over in a matter of seconds as the Aurora races toward them at almost Mach 8.

The Aurora's pilot suddenly sees the missiles' smoke trail directly in front of him. With the aircraft's threat alert system screaming in his ear, he realizes the game is up.

I might as well be remembered as a RAFCO martyr, he thinks and pulls the trigger.

The locking pins on the Aurora's missile bay doors retract and the hydraulic rams forcefully push the doors open into the high wind screaming under the aircraft. The underbelly rack automatically releases the first P-500 nuclear tipped supersonic cruise missile. After falling almost two hundred feet, the cruise missile's engine bursts to life. Shooting fire and smoke more than seventy-five feet behind its tail section, the missile begins to accelerate, following its preprogrammed course.

The Aurora does not survive the next moment. Multiple AIM-120C missiles penetrate her fuselage, slicing their way deep into her structure. Several more missiles explode only a few feet from the Aurora's skin, spraying hundreds of red-hot metallic shards over the cockpit, wings and vertical fins.

Within microseconds, the fuel compartment is breached and the rapidly escaping methane gas ignites from the heat generated by the missile impacts. The Aurora explodes, opening up and releasing its inner structural guts like road kill on a hot summer day.

All six Bravo squadron F-22s see the size and intensity of the explosion and believe their mission is successful. The view of the detonation cloud brings to mind thoughts of that sad January day in 1986, when the Space Shuttle Challenger exploded on ascent, not far from their current location.

But, today is not that day. Today is a good day, Major Sutherland thinks. *The evil has been contained.*

Reaper Two-Six
Year 6

The F-22's fuel consumption while in maximum afterburner flight mode is massive, so Major Sutherland orders his men to pull back on their throttles. With their fuel supply dwindling quickly, and with no tanker in the air, Bravo squadron needs to conserve as much fuel as possible in order to return safely to a nearby base. There is no way the F-22s will make it back to Tyndall, so Major Sutherland directs his squadron toward one of the bases near Jacksonville, Florida. If the fuel situation becomes critical, the squadron can land at an even closer civilian airport. Once safely on the ground, the F-22s will refuel and fly back to their home base in Tyndall.

"Sir," one of Major Sutherland's wingmen says. "We've got a smoke trail leaving the debris cloud. It appears to be smaller than an aircraft, but clearly visible and accelerating northward. I don't have it on radar yet due to the clutter from the explosion."

Major Sutherland stretches his neck and turns to his left, spotting the missile's smoke trail. *What in the hell is that?*

Chapter 21
The Twin Sun

Climbing to 158,400 feet, the cruise missile continues northward toward its target — Washington D.C., nearly seven hundred miles away. The missile's 350-kiloton nuclear bomb is tightly packed into its nose section, awaiting the detonation signal from its inertial navigation system. With the missile whistling through the atmosphere at more than fourteen hundred knots, the eastern coast of the United States is less than twenty-six minutes from plunging back into the dark ages.

If the high altitude nuclear bomb explodes, a powerful EMP burst will be unleashed, with the capability to destroy the electrical grid for more than five hundred miles in all directions from the point of detonation. As the effects cascade from region to region, the power systems throughout most of the United States will become overloaded, shutting down as breaker after breaker begins to trip.

The severe lack of electrical power replacement components will obliterate the very fabric of today's modern society for years. In the first few weeks after the permanent blackouts, millions will perish due to lack of food and clean water, followed by millions more dying from disease and environmental conditions months later. The population of the United States could easily shrink by more than ninety percent in less than a year.

From the Oval Office, the President alerts the Pentagon and NORAD, along with numerous military installations up-and-down the east coast of the United States. All track the hostile cruise missile.

Navy Carrier Strike Group Two Commander Rear Admiral Kate Thomson has now joined the teleconference with President Mason, Secretary Dow, Wolverine, and a few other high-ranking leaders from other military installations.

Even though the missile's payload is unknown, President Mason and those on the teleconference assume it is a nuclear warhead. As the missile rapidly approaches the Carolina coast, a hysterical panic rants out of the speakerphone and begins to overshadow the entire discussion.

Wolverine is determined to stop the political bickering he's hearing. He refuses to let it drag him down, or keep him from focusing on what's important.

Intently fixated on the front screen, Red Diamond displays the hostile missile's actual as well as projected flight path.

Shooting down a target moving at Mach 2.5 is tough enough, but knocking it out of the sky thirty miles up, that's nearly impossible, Wolverine thinks.

As he wracks his brain for a solution, deep worry lines crease his face.

The teleconference quickly turns into a frenzied debate over which conventional defensive system should be launched. Secretary Dow wants to use the Patriot missiles stationed at Fort Bragg, North Carolina, or even a fighter launched missile out of Langley, Virginia. Rear Admiral Thomson opts for the cruiser based RIM-67 extended range surface-to-air missiles. The President is ready to approve all three methods to ensure they destroy the hostile missile.

Wolverine keeps shaking his head in dismay thinking, *Hell ... no conventional system can destroy something that high. That's almost halfway into space. They've got to know those will not work. The target is too damn high. The President is grasping at straws ... I guess he's got to try something. What about ...?*

Wolverine's expression suddenly goes blank, but his brain fires hot neurons. *Oh come on,* he thinks, trying to recall the name of the system he worked on before joining the GDO. He turns and refocuses his attention on the laptop staring at him in the face. After punching in a few keys, he scans the screen and finally says, "That's it — the AEGIS Ballistic Missile Defense system."

The Navy was testing newly developed RIM-161 missiles to use as their front line defensive system. More commonly known as the SM-3 missile, it is designed to intercept hostile ballistic missiles at extremely high altitudes; the system also has anti-satellite capabilities. The SM-3 uses a hit-to-kill high energy kinetic warhead to disable the target's threat.

"Rear Admiral Thomson," Wolverine says. "Is the SM-3 system operational?"

"It is," she says, as the bickering subsides. "But that's for near Earth orbiting threats. How will that …?"

Suddenly she realizes that everyone is focusing on the threat as a conventional nuclear cruise missile. But at its current thirty mile altitude, none of the standard United States' defensive weapons will be able to reach it.

"Mr. President," she says, her voice firm with a no-nonsense tone. "I'm in agreement with Wolverine. We need to consider our response to the hostile more in terms of how we would respond to an inbound ballistic missile."

"Can the SM-3s reach the target in time?" President Mason asks.

The tension over the phone mounts, and Wolverine senses the blame game rearing its ugly head, the result of the muffled side conversations he hears through the phone.

Jesus, he thinks. *The United States is under imminent attack and all they can think about is saving their own asses from the fallout. For Christ's sake, is there anyone over there with a full set of balls?*

Rear Admiral Thomson replies: "The SM-3 is fast enough and can easily reach the target's current altitude. I realize that atmospheric intercept is not its intended purpose, but it is probably our best shot."

The President consults with his cabinet, then asks, "Do you have a SM-3 boat near the hostile's path?"

Rear Admiral Thomson tilts her head to the right and pinches the phone between her shoulder and ear. Entering a few keystrokes into her computer and scanning a few screens-worth of data, she finally says, "The only SM-3 boat near the hostile missile's projected flight path just left port from Charleston. All my east coast warships are monitoring the situation, so they should be able to launch within minutes."

After a final poll of his cabinet members, the President orders the strike. "Do it, Admiral. Get that bird in the air."

Reaper Two-Six
Year 6

"Yes, Mr. President," she says, picking up the phone to the Captain of the USS Tuxpan.

One of the Navy's front line Ticonderoga class warships, the Tuxpan is outfitted with the latest missile systems. With a length approaching six hundred feet and a crew close to four hundred sailors, the multi-role guided missile warships are an integral part of the Navy's Carrier Battle Group.

Within seconds, the Tuxpan's Captain orders the weapons officer to activate the AEGIS primary air warfare defensive system. Four powerful three-dimensional phased array search and tracking radars immediately begin panning the skies for the rogue RAFCO missile.

The advanced large-screen LCD weapon control stations located in the warship's combat information center glow to life. Each station operator quickly and skillfully manipulates the vast quantity of buttons, dials and switches in front of them.

Once the Tuxpan's system locks onto the hostile cruise missile, it begins streaming data to the fire control system to determine a targeting solution. Less than a minute later, the SM-3 vertical launching missile system is activated.

The Captain of the Tuxpan checks with his senior officers to ensure all is ready, and then orders the launch.

Reaper Two-Six
Year 6

The SM-3's solid-fuel rocket engine ignites, shooting flames over thirty feet into the air near the bow of the ship. The powerful rocket engine forces the missile out of its vertical launching system tube, beginning its intercept course for the RAFCO cruise missile more than a hundred-twenty miles away.

Being an AEGIS capable warship, the target tracking system encompasses a comprehensive sea and land-based radar network. Once airborne, the SM-3 missile establishes communication with the Tuxpan's fire control system for any necessary course corrections.

Only a few minutes into the flight, the SM-3's booster burns out and separates, allowing the dual-thrust second stage rocket motor to propel the interceptor missile throughout the remainder of its atmospheric trajectory. The missile continues to receive updated guidance information from the launching ship, along with its own GPS navigational system.

The RAFCO cruise missile passes over the South Carolina coast, just east of Myrtle Beach. Still blistering through the air at Mach 2.5, the cruise missile is closing in on the capital of the United States — now less than four hundred miles away.

Soaring through the sky at over five thousand knots, the SM-3 intercept missile rapidly closes the distance to its target. Within seconds of unleashing its kinetic warhead, the SM-3's onboard sensors begin to probe the target, attempting to identify the most lethal part of the RAFCO cruise missile.

The teleconference becomes dead silent as all eyes lock onto the video screens, where readouts of the second-by-second drama unfold thirty miles above the Carolina coastal region. The severity of the situation is boldly written on everyone's face.

As the SM-3's GPS-Aided Inertial Navigation System evaluates the target, it finally releases its kinetic warhead from the nosecone. More than fourteen pounds of TNT equivalent explosives are packed into a successful direct hit, shredding anything in its path, and hopefully permanently disabling the cruise missile.

The warhead glides effortlessly through the sky as it zips toward the cruise missile's guidance computer section. Powerful long range cameras try desperately to maintain focus on the impending impact, transmitting its live video feed to everyone on the teleconference. The tension of each person reaches a volatile point.

Seconds later, the nose of the cruise missile appears to take a hit from a bright reflective object — the kinetic warhead. The cruise missile shudders and then abruptly turns eastward, not appearing to be severely damaged. The guidance control system is partially disabled by the impact of the kinetic warhead, causing the RAFCO cruise missile to veer off-target and head east.

"Shit, it was just a glancing blow," mutters one of the President's cabinet members.

The Secretary of Homeland Security asks, "Should we notify Emergency Services, Mr. President?"

"And tell them what?" President Mason asks. "That we need to evacuate millions of people, and by doing so incite mass panic? We don't even know what to prepare them for: a dud sick joke missile to get us to expose our response capabilities so they can strike us again harder at a future date? An EMP strike, and if this were an EMP strike, do we know how widespread or powerful it might be? What would we be evacuating them from, nuclear fallout?

"No," President Mason continues. "As much as I hate to do nothing, I see no real choice, ladies and gentleman. We'll know in less than seven minutes how severe the situation will be. I want all agencies on immediate alert, ready to move out at a moment's notice."

Dozens of voices erupt at the same time as cabinet members frantically attempt to contact their respective high-level officers. The monitors continue to show live video footage of the cruise missile's easterly path, just crossing the Cape Hatteras barrier islands.

At least it's offshore now, Wolverine thinks, noticing the tension easing over the teleconference. *Maybe we'll catch a break after all, and this thing will run out of fuel and fall harmlessly to the bottom of the Atlantic. I'll take anything right now to prevent a catastrophe.*

As the moments tick by, all eyes focus on the live video footage from the long-range camera. Wolverine glances at the upper left hand corner of his large LCD screen, staring intently at the cruise missile's speed, altitude and directional information from both land and satellite radar signals.

It has to be getting low on fuel, he thinks. *Either it's going to drop out of the sky or ... oh, no!*

The intense light from the 350-kiloton nuclear cruise missile detonation temporarily blinds the TV screens. The fiery red-orange glowing ball of flame rapidly expands in the low density high-altitude air. From the Carolina shoreline, the eastern sky suddenly shines with the brightness of two suns: one beautiful, warm and full of life energy ... the other ugly, fierce and full of destruction.

Reaper Two-Six
Year 6

A violent burst of electromagnetic radiation slams into the stratosphere, ripping atomic particles out of the upper atmospheric molecules. The highly energized and ionized particles stream downward at nearly the speed of light, showering everything in its path with a vicious electromagnetic pulse.

Moments later, the data and video feed monitoring the cruise missile abruptly goes dead. Wolverine's heart sinks with the unthinkable … *No!*

Chapter 22
The Rain of Evil
East of Cape Hatteras, North Carolina, United States

As the atomic cloud begins dissipating over the Atlantic Ocean, the remnants will make their way toward Europe. In less than twenty-four hours, radioactive particles catching a ride on the jet stream will rain down on Ireland, Norway, Sweden, Denmark, the United Kingdom, and the rest of northern Europe. Most effects of the nuclear bomb won't be apparent for years or even decades, as the radioactive induced cellular damage manifests itself throughout humanity as well as the animal and plant kingdoms.

The United States and Bermuda are assaulted in a different manner. Minutes after the bomb's explosion, the potent EMP strike flashed through the air, striking at nearly everything capable of conducting magnetic or electrical power. The rain of an EMP burst stalls automobiles without warning; aircraft become aluminum tubes of death; high-rise office buildings turn into ghost pillars of steel and glass; any computer or modern electronic equipment not well shielded will eventually find the trash bin or be recycled for scrap. Life after a massive EMP more closely resembles the sixteenth century colonies than today's brightly lit neon cities.

The epicenter of the nuclear detonation, situated three hundred miles east of Cape Hatteras, completely decimates Bermuda's power grid. The British owned territory of more than sixty-five thousand residents and tourists soon begin its first night in total darkness, enduring the stifling August heat and punishing humidity. Sweat-drenched clothing clinging to every inch of their bodies will become an everyday occurrence for the inhabitants of the mid-Atlantic colony. Isolated thousands of miles away from countries that can help and now without power, Bermuda's new monetary system will evolve around bartering for clean water, food, and basic medical supplies. Looting, disease, gangs, and deadly crimes of all types are sure to run amok in the small island country.

More than half of North Carolina is in the same situation as Bermuda. The central and eastern parts are completely without power, along with southeastern Virginia and eastern South Carolina. Washington D.C., spared a direct hit by the EMP, was able to move quickly. Government officials implemented an action plan to get emergency power to the eight affected nuclear power plants. In addition, the military received orders to provide security and to support

mandatory evacuations of all affected areas to temporary
shelters.

Sure feels like Katrina all over again, a national
guardsman thinks as he loads food and supplies onto a
transport pallet. *What the hell happened in Carolina?*
They're not telling us shit.

Modern nuclear power plants are designed with an
emergency shutdown or SCRAM capability. In the event of a
full power failure, the reactor is automatically SCRAM'd. To
achieve this, large neutron-absorbing control rods are
inserted into the nuclear core automatically by gravitational
and mechanical spring forces. The nuclear reaction is then
halted by the neutron grabbing rods.

When the EMP struck the eastern part of the United
States, it was assumed that the nuclear power plants'
automatic SCRAM system worked properly. Without the
availability of electrical instrumentation, the power plant
operators have no way to ensure the public is protected from
a tragic nuclear event. Therefore, as a precautionary measure,
the manager ordered all employees to leave the premises,
adding confusion to an already delicate situation.

The general population has no idea that an EMP
strike has occurred; they see only its destructive results: no
air or rail travel, no cell phones, no Internet, no TV, no street

or traffic lights. Basically, there is no electrical power, backup generators do not work, and automobiles sit stalled everywhere. The first few hours after an EMP event are critical in maintaining civil order because mass confusion and chaos threaten to erupt into riots at any moment.

Ironically, the warship USS Tuxpan that launched the SM-3 missile is a casualty of the EMP strike, floating adrift and without power just east of Charleston. The Captain orders general quarters for all hands. This is a familiar order for all military installations and ships in the affected region. Norfolk, a major naval facility, is dead silent for the first time in its nearly century long existence.

Communities between a hundred-fifty and two hundred miles from the Carolina and Virginia coasts are mostly unaffected by the EMP blast, so citizens in the affected zones will be evacuated and transported to these nearby locations. Military and emergency services load food, water and medical suppliers onto aircraft and trucks for delivery and distribution to the affected residents. Although the intercept was technically a failure, the SM-3 prevented the RAFCO cruise missile from reaching its intended target, saving the lives of millions of Americans.

As the United States seeks to provide stability to the affected regions, the GDO continues to focus on its mission to eradicate as many members of the RAFCO organization from existence as possible.

In the Netherlands, PVL's daughter, Samantha, greatly concerned that her father's condition is more serious than stomach flu, decides to take her father to a local minor emergency clinic as he was experiencing frequent vomiting and diarrhea for hours. After running a number of tests, the doctors diagnose him with food poisoning. Treating him with intravenous fluids and antibiotics, he is finally able to return home the next morning with strict doctor's orders for bed rest, clear fluids, and the necessary prescription medications.

Later that day, PVL's strength begins to improve, so he decides to review his messages. Already illuminated on his laptop is a message indicating activity on his private FTP site.

Even in his severely weakened condition, PVL is angered, and says, "Fucking hackers."

The thought of Doc and Professor never enters his mind as it has been more than six months since his last contact with them.

PVL nearly decides to ignore the message, lacking the energy to deal with the fallout of his account potentially being hacked. However, he reluctantly logs onto the FTP site.

"What in the …" he mutters.

Moments later, the flabbergasted and stunned look on PVL's face tells the whole story. He is elated to hear from Doc and Professor. Once he opened the 'read me' file, the document nearly took PVL's breath away. He is horrified by RAFCO's plan.

"I knew they were an evil organization," he says. "But this? They were planning multiple EMP strikes over several weeks, and even months, in a quest to destabilize the United States and European Union. Holy shit!"

He wipes a hand over his eyes and forwards the data to Wolverine. He follows up minutes later with a phone call.

When Wolverine answers, PVL apologizes for his absence and for the delay in sending the intel. They speak for nearly an hour, discussing the events of the previous twenty-four hours.

After the call, PVL, too keyed up to rest, groans, "I've been incapacitated too long. It's time to get back in the loop."

He knows that if his daughter catches him at his desk so soon after his illness, he'll never hear the end of it; so he unplugs his laptop and takes it in with him into the bedroom. As he settles into his bed with the computer, he smiles. Even if she nags him, he is grateful to have such a loving daughter.

Soon, as he begins to catch up on the situation at hand, his thoughts drift away from his sickness and the comfort his daughter's care brought to him over the last several weeks. He immerses himself in the current situation and quickly his thoughts drift to Doc and Professor, hoping against all hope that they are still alive.

RAFCO HQ, Colombia

Earlier in the day, the Aurora rocketed out of the runway tunnel at the RAFCO HQ. Once the residual heat and ear deafening reverberations from its engines subsided, Doc was able to quietly make her way to the end of tunnel. After trudging along for more than a mile inside the dreary underground runway, Doc finally appears on the back side of the mountain.

Ah, she thinks as the morning sunshine glistens off her sweaty skin. *Freedom!*

She closes her eyes and soaks up the warmth beaming down upon her, enjoying a calm moment for the first time in more than six months. She looks and feels like a beat-up rag doll, tattered and dirt-smeared. Not even the humidity, which has increased two-fold since the rain, can diminish her pleasure in the moment.

The abandoned highway, now used by RAFCO as a secret runway, continues in the old valley pass for almost another mile before vanishing again into another tunnel system.

She squints into the sun, scanning the surrounding vicinity and evaluating her options. Focusing on the southbound area, she thinks. *Okay, Professor, don't forget about me.*

Understanding the plan is for Professor to meet her in the stolen Hummer, Doc decides that she better continue to walk on roadways. *Relatively clear ones too, if possible,* she thinks, realizing that she could be more easily spotted by a RAFCO search party. *I'll just have to take that chance,* she concludes. *If I want to get out of here alive, Professor is my only hope.*

On the other side of the mountain, Professor floors the gas pedal of the Hummer and successfully speeds down RAFCO's main runway unscathed. He weaves the entire mile and a half, blazing past anyone and everything that attempts to keep him from his goal — freedom. As he approaches the far end of the runway, he slams on the brakes and skids into a hard right turn.

Eyeing the front gate, he mumbles, "Freedom, I have you now."

Whistling along at almost seventy-five mph, the front grill of the Hummer makes quick work of the barrier and smashes through the camp's simple chained gate.

Of course, it only has a single chain. It's not as if they have any nasty neighbors they're trying to keep out. RAFCO is the nasty neighbor.

Professor carefully looks toward the sun to get his bearings, and ponders, *I have to head northward, somehow. Don't worry, Doc, I'm on my way. I'll find you. Somehow, I'll find you ... somehow ...*

Chapter 23
Redemption
Carnarvon, Western Australia

Several hours after the destruction of the Aurora, Wolverine sits in his office at the Australian GDO center. His eyes narrow as he thinks about Esteban, the leader of the RAFCO terrorist group. *You failed Esteban ... You failed.*

His lips form a single line as he continues to focus on the dozens of image files streaming from the attachments PVL sent.

"Damn," he mumbles. "Doc and Professor were busy these past few months." He continues to scan through the intel taken during their stay in the RAFCO compound.

Wolverine grins, "Nicely done."

A few minutes later, Wolverine overhears a discussion from the main control room. Needing a break from scrutinizing all the data bombarding his brain, he gets up and makes his way down the narrow hallway. Immediately, the front screen draws his attention: it clearly shows the current situation of Professor and Doc in Colombia.

Not long ago, the X-47s were finally given clearance to fly over the RAFCO HQ after the Storm Reapers' squadron disposed of the patrolling J-20s. Nodding his head in approval, Wolverine allows himself a smile; the first real one in many days now that he knows Professor and Doc are alive and well.

The two X-47s circle the RAFCO HQ in a coordinated pattern, using their powerful imaging systems to expose the locations of all personnel in and around the camp. One X-47 spotted Professor in a vehicle speeding around curves on a mountainous road just north-northeast of RAFCO's HQ. The other saw Doc dart across an old highway, several miles northeast of the main camp.

Wolverine thinks about the local terrain. *How did she get that far away from the camp? That is some of the roughest terrain in the world.*

Aloud he says, "Damn impressive, Doc. I can't wait for this debriefing."

Red Diamond looks up at the Admiral, grins, and says, "I think this is going to be more like a celebration, isn't it?"

Wolverine nods in agreement, "You're right, Red, I was certain that one or both of them were dead. Those are two tough Reapers. That's for sure."

Reaper Two-Six
Year 6

"You bet," Red Diamond says as he bumps fists with
Wolverine. "Grit and determination, isn't that a Reaper
prerequisite?"

They chuckle, as they look at the screen, still unable
to believe that two of their own made it into and out of such a
hostile environment, without backup support from them.

Washington DC, United States

From the Oval Office in the West Wing of the White
House, President Mason addresses the nation, and the world,
via TV, radio and the Internet:

"My fellow citizens, today, we were awakened by
evil, and we were called upon to defend freedom. The United
States of America was suddenly and deliberately attacked by
a global terrorist organization known as RAFCO.

"This morning, at 10:14 Eastern Standard Time, a
nuclear device detonated high over the Atlantic Ocean,
approximately three hundred miles east of Cape Hatteras.
With the combined efforts of the Air Force, Navy, and the
Global Defense Organization, the United States avoided an
almost certain tragic situation."

"Shit. He would have to bring up the GDO,"
Secretary Mallory grumbles while he watches the President's
address with Secretary Dow at the Area 51 HQ building.

"The fuckers are going to get all the credit again. I just know it. Christ!"

The President's speech continues: "We were not completely spared from the effects of the nuclear bomb, as a powerful EMP impacted parts of our eastern shoreline, cutting power to many local communities. Tonight, our hearts, our prayers, and our support go out to the citizens living in the eastern parts of Virginia, North and South Carolina, the areas most severely impacted.

"With the support of our military and numerous disaster preparedness organizations, we are already beginning to bring emergency power to the affected regions, as well as providing necessary transportation to the Red Cross' temporary shelters. Within forty-eight hours, I expect all Americans affected by the EMP will have a hot meal and a secure place to rest their head. We will show the world that America does not live in fear. We will endure and will bring our enemies to justice."

Near RAFCO HQ, Colombia

Just north of the RAFCO HQ, Professor drives the stolen Hummer like a man possessed. Two objectives consume his thoughts: find Doc and get the hell out of this jungle, to freedom.

Reaper Two-Six
Year 6

Professor sees a stream of water crossing the roadway, runoff from the earlier storm, and slows for a curve in the road. The tires slide, causing the vehicle to fishtail, and he nearly careens off the edge.

Regaining control of the vehicle, he makes the turn and finally spots Doc up ahead. He floors the gas pedal for the remaining four hundred yards, and then slams on the brakes, screeching to a complete stop along side of her.

Always a smart ass, Professor tries to brighten Doc's spirits, with his playful banter.

"Hi, gorgeous. Fancy meeting a pretty lady like you out here," Professor says with the sexiest wink and grin he can muster.

"Can I give you a lift into town? I'd love to buy you a drink and show you my war wounds," he adds, pointing to the pseudo tourniquet on his arm.

Doc grins in spite of herself. "Really, that's the best you can come up with?"

"Hey, I did the best I could." He laughs as she jumps into the Hummer and slams the door.

"Just get us out of here, okay?" she says.

Smiling from ear to ear, Professor nods and says, "I'm glad you're all right."

They decide to head north, for the coast. Professor once more guns the motor and looks ahead as the tires spin gravel and loose dirt into a cloud of dust behind them.

Shortly thereafter, they hear the roar of aircraft buzzing overhead.

Washington DC, United States

President Mason's speech carries on: "By their unprovoked actions, our enemies have shown us no mercy and offered us no respect.

"As Commander in Chief of the Armed Forces, I've ordered all measures be taken for our defense. I believe Congress and the American people will agree that we must not only defend ourselves, but we must ensure this form of treachery can never endanger us, or any other nation ever again. No matter how long this may take, the American people will enjoy absolute victory."

Carnarvon, Western Australia

A cruise missile attack is an act of war, so the President of the United States uses his executive powers to authorize military force against RAFCO. Wolverine watches his small laptop screen as more than a dozen Navy and Reaper fighters bomb RAFCO's HQ, leveling the camp.

Near RAFCO HQ, Colombia

Professor and Doc continue to make their way northward; behind them, in the direction of the RAFCO camp, they hear numerous loud bomb detonations.

It had to be done, Doc thinks. *The evil was too prevalent ... and getting too strong.*

Several miles away, the magnitude of the explosions emanating from the RAFCO HQ is overwhelming. *Guess there'll be nothing but a crater after today,* Professor muses, recalling last year's failed attempt.

Washington DC, United States

The President's speech is nearly finished now. He concludes by saying, "Our support for global peace must reach beyond the American borders, it must reach beyond all borders on Earth if it is to succeed. Six years ago, the United States committed to support the fight on international terrorism by spearheading the creation of the Global Defense Organization, also known as the GDO.

"I am here today to reaffirm my strong support, both financial and political, for this important multinational anti-terrorist organization. I encourage, no I insist, that all the leaders of the world who are serious about fighting terrorism join us in supporting the GDO.

"We will come together as one global community to promote stability, to strengthen our intelligence capabilities, to give law enforcement the additional tools they need, and to take active steps that strengthen the world's economy. We must never forget that if terror goes unpunished, it will threaten the stability of all legitimate governments."

Near RAFCO HQ, Colombia

While piloting his F-22 after a bombing run over the RAFCO HQ, Viral enters a steep northerly banking turn and spots a Hummer. Believing it is the same vehicle the X-47 spotted earlier, he decides to signal the occupants.

Viral pulls back on the throttle and drops to less than three hundred feet. Heading straight for the Hummer, he buzzes it at two hundred, sixty knots while rolling his wings alternating left side up, right side down and vice-versa. After several wing rolls, he pulls a hard 180-degree turn and takes another pass over the vehicle.

Recognizing the signal and seeing the Reaper logo shining brightly off the aircraft's fuselage, Professor stops the vehicle, gets out and waves at the pilot of the F-22. Overhead, Viral repeats the wing rolls again. A smile finally spreads across Viral's face. *That's them all right, and they're alive!* Viral radios their position to Captain Shaw on the USS Carl Vinson.

Doc lowers her head and covers her face with her hands. Relief spreads through her like a warm bath and she is close to tears.

It's over, it's finally over, she thinks.

She rarely allows her emotions to show, but the overwhelming stress of the past several months is too much. Now, finally, she feels relief; the floodgates open, and she loses her composure. She lets a few tears seep from the corner of each eye.

Professor lets her have a moment while she releases some of her pent up emotions.

However, he can't give her too long — they now face the task of getting out of this jungle and back to someone, anyone, in the GDO. They continue their trek toward the coast in hopes that there will soon be a friendly ship anchored offshore or a chopper overhead, ready to take them to safety.

They both think of one word almost in tandem, *home,* an improbability a few days ago.

Reaper Two-Six
Year 6

Carnarvon, Western Australia

At the GDO center in Australia, Wolverine finds an interesting document contained in the files from PVL. It appears that RAFCO had some serious ties with Korea.

Hmmm ... he ponders. *I wonder if the communist North Koreans became RAFCO's financial and weapons source after China dried up.*

After today's events and the President's commitment, Wolverine believes there is nothing to worry about — RAFCO is dead or will be shortly.

Wolverine uses the remote control to click off the television, after the President's speech finished. He slowly sits back in his corner chair. A soothing and relaxing calm begins to settle over him.

It's done ... Like Jorge Valdez, your reign of terror has finally ended under my watchful eyes. Goodbye, Esteban Bertiz. You and your evil minions are gone from the face of the Earth.

Chapter 24
Freedom's Price
NATO+ HQ, Brussels, Belgium

Doc's eyes glaze over as she remembers the day nearly three weeks ago … the day she was freed from RAFCO's rule and plucked out of the Columbian jungle by a helicopter from the aircraft carrier USS Carl Vinson. Now, her freedom faces a new threat, not by a terrorist group but by the United States government.

"Do you have anything else to add, Captain?" a loud voice booms out of the loudspeakers, echoing off the walls of the large room.

Doc's gaze locks onto the notes in front of her; her mind keeps replaying that helicopter extraction scene over and over again. The right side of her mouth curls into half a smile because, at the time, she thought she was finally going home, *home.*

"Captain?" echoes loudly throughout the room.

Doc blinks, looks up, and says, "No, nothing more to add."

"Thank you, Captain, you may step down," Naomi says. After the assassination of Elena Filatov, Naomi Walker was appointed as President of NATO+ almost a year ago.

Naomi is an imposing figure. But to Wolverine, she doesn't have the humanity or unspoken compassion that Elena had. Wolverine has no doubt that she will be a good President, but in his heart, he believes no one can replace Elena.

The highest governing NATO+ authoritative body, the Council, is currently chaired by Naomi Walker.

Doc steps down from the witness stand and walks toward the back of the room. Her eyes drift upward to the beautiful mural covering the entire back wall behind her. Placed with precision directly in the center of the mural is the iconic NATO+ symbol ... a symbol she's only previously seen on formal GDO communications until today. The new design for the NATO+ symbol incorporated the original NATO design of a dark blue flag with a white compass rose emblem and the radiating four white lines.

Doc reaches her seat and sits. Professor, sitting on her left, throws her a wink and a smile, trying to communicate to her that it'll be all right. She grimaces and returns his glance with a forced partial smile of her own.

"Not really the way I wanted to see the headquarters," she whispers to Professor.

She sighs, takes a few deep breaths, shakes her head slowly, and adds, "I just hope this isn't the last thing I get to see as a free woman."

Doc looks at Wolverine and PVL, sitting to her right. Her half-hearted smile shows the agony tearing apart her soul.

Their mission to bring down RAFCO was a success, but the success could also come at a price — Doc and Professor's freedom. Now, the very decisions they made to infiltrate RAFCO's camp, which led to the successful elimination of the terrorist group, are under scrutiny to determine if they are to face criminal charges.

Fifty-two members of the NATO+ council sit around a very large circular table in the center of the room. The remaining forty-four NATO+ partner members sit in neat rows along a sidewall. The back wall, *the wall of shame,* Professor joked, is a single row of chairs with a makeshift podium style witness stand positioned at the end, near the corner.

For this formal hearing, all members who require translation wear headsets. The witness stand microphone broadcasts the testimony throughout the council room and the small adjoining rooms, where translators support NATO+ members.

"Fleet Admiral Wolverine, do you have any final remarks before the council makes their decision?" Naomi says in a firm tone.

Wolverine notices a familiar tone in Naomi's voice; a tone that reminds him of Elena. He always appreciated Elena's composure and honesty, but her real strength was in the power of her spoken words. Her voice, tone and carefully chosen words are what allowed Elena to rise with such speed and influence, all the while with tremendous respect.

Wolverine nods and gets to his feet. His crisp formal GDO uniform, similar in style to the U.S. Navy dress uniform, neatly drapes his husky six-foot frame. His normally tan and healthy glow now reflects the emotional and physical toll of the past few weeks; his face is drawn and pale.

He walks to the stand, hopeful that Naomi and the council will understand the importance of the mission and the GDO. Nothing she said or did specifically told Wolverine that she supports the GDO, but something intangible speaks to him, something in her mannerisms, her voice, her attitude throughout this entire proceeding.

She could have immediately demanded the resignation of PVL, Doc and Professor, before turning them over to the U.S. military courts. As their commander, she could easily have ordered the same for him.

Wolverine sighs heavily and thinks, *And it's within her rights to do so.*

However, curiously, and much to his surprise, she didn't. She wanted and demanded to hear for herself the reasons behind the decisions made throughout the mission, in order to develop a deep understanding of what happened at the RAFCO camp.

Wolverine steps up to the witness stand and catches a glimpse of the wall to his right, where all ninety-six-member flags hang. The most recent addition, China, brings a pleasing smile to his face.

No matter what today's outcome, he thinks, *I am grateful for the chance to serve the world in such a vital capacity. We* have *made a difference. The presence of that flag is proof.*

As the six-plus hour marathon hearing nears an end, Wolverine offers a final thanks to the council for their time and that he feels confident they will use respect and fairness as they deliberate the fate of the members of the GDO. He reassures them that the seriousness of the GDO's actions is no light matter to him, and he pledges they will strictly follow the council's verdict.

Both Professor and Doc swallow hard as visions of a new Leavenworth home dance in their minds. They exchange a quick solemn glance at each other.

Wolverine finishes his speech, respectfully reminding the council of the GDO's charter, and shares a few of their previous successes. He then personally thanks Noami before stepping down and returning to his seat against the back wall.

Doc reaches over and touches Wolverine softly on the hand. "Thank you," she says.

This isn't the first time Wolverine exceeded her expectations as a leader. *He had nothing to do with the mission ... nothing ... but here he sits defending our honor, our actions, our asses as if they are his own,* she ponders.

Wolverine insisted that if his Reapers stood accused of anything, then he stood accused as well. Doc has learned to trust Wolverine with her very life, and has always felt secure these past five plus years in the knowledge he would do everything in his power to bring her home safe on every mission, including this one, where he had no prior knowledge.

The court guards escort the Reapers to the bathroom for a break, then take them to a waiting room while the council deliberates. All four Reapers immediately fall into their chairs, exhausted. A moment later, the door opens and a waiter pushes a wheeled cart full of small sandwiches, a selection of various pastries, a pitcher of water, some cookies, and a full pot of coffee into the room. The waiter turns toward the Reapers, smiles, and excuses himself, closing the door firmly behind him.

The air in the waiting room weighs heavy with an eerie silence. All four Reapers know the time for words is gone, and they all reflect privately on the possible outcome of the hearing.

In stark contrast, the deliberation in the council room is bustling with activity and noise. The decision must be unanimous by the NATO+ Council, there are no majority rules for these trials. Naomi, as Chairperson and President of NATO+, is responsible for negotiating with the fifty-two full members to obtain total consensus.

As the waiting minutes turn into hours, the exhaustion and emotional stress are too much; all four Reapers succumb to an early evening nap in their quiet room. While their bodies and minds recharge, their fate nears a conclusion. Naomi is preparing the final version of their judgment for proof reading and then approval by all council members.

Forty-five minutes later, Wolverine, PVL, Doc and Professor return to the council room. They remain standing in front of their seats as Naomi addresses them.

Reaper Two-Six
Year 6

"It's late, so I'll get right down to business," she begins.

Wolverine has always appreciated a person willing to be direct, yet diplomatic. He unconsciously nods in agreement for her to proceed.

Continuing, Naomi looks down at the document in front of her on the table and reads aloud, "On the count of treason against the United States … this Council finds Doc and Professor guilty."

Doc's heart sinks as her eyes slowly gaze at Professor.

"As their direct commanding officers, PVL and Wolverine are herby found guilty of accessory to treason," Naomi adds.

A look of utter disbelief crosses Doc's face. She reaches up and covers her mouth while turning toward Wolverine and PVL.

"No, they did nothing to deserve this," she mumbles. A pain courses through the pit of her stomach. She crosses her arms over her mid-section and bows her head slightly in response to the pain.

A long pause sweeps throughout the NATO+ Council room. A few moments later, Naomi lifts her head to face the Reapers and says, "However."

Reaper Two-Six
Year 6

"There's a however?" Doc whispers, cocking an eyebrow.

Naomi continues in a more pleasing tone. "Since all charges are from the United States, and taking into consideration the recent events leading to removal of RAFCO as a global terrorist organization, not to mention your involvement in preventing a potential nuclear catastrophe, President Mason is prepared to offer a full pardon."

Doc's jaw drops as a single tear of joy trickles from her right eye.

Naomi explains. "There are conditions attached to the President's pardon … They are:

"One, Wolverine will be demoted to Admiral. Two, PVL will be demoted to Vice Admiral. And three, the GDO will no longer report directly to me, but will now be a division of the NATO+ military committee. The GDO will report directly to Admiral Anthony Bell, Chairman of the NATO+ Military Committee. All activities will require prior approval from Admiral Bell. Four, the GDO HQ will be relocated from Michigan to the current GDO Eastern Command in Stavoren, Netherlands. The two remaining GDO command centers will be shut down permanently. Finally, five, Doc and Professor will resign from the GDO."

Doc gasps.

"As restitution for the property lost by the United States — namely the Aurora — Doc and Professor will be assigned to support the activities at Area 51 and report to Colonel Landis," Naomi finishes.

Her green eyes burn with determination as she looks at Doc and Professor, and she firmly adds, "I want to be completely clear about what is expected. One complaint about your behavior while at Area 51 could be enough to get you put behind bars, and I want to add that Colonel Landis is not pleased about 'babysitting' the two of you.

"So you'd better find a way to make the situation work for everyone involved. The only reason the Colonel agreed to this is that the Department of Defense ordered him to improve Area 51's security and flight test programs. And, your firsthand experience in these areas caught the fancy of President Mason."

Noami drops her eyes to glance at the stack of papers before her, and then continues, her tone sincere. "After a year of dedicated service to the United States, the GDO can petition the Secretary of Defense for your return to active duty with Reaper Two-Six."

Reaper Two-Six
Year 6

Naomi sits back in her chair to show she's finished with her speech. The air in the room settles into an almost ghostly stillness.

Without hesitation, Wolverine snaps his heals together, stands at attention, and announces, "Madam President. We accept all conditions and thank you for your efforts on our behalf."

Professor stares blazingly at him. "I'm not resigning from the GDO. Hell, without me, RAFCO could be taking over half the U.S. by now. They should be thanking me," he snorts under his breath.

Wolverine waves a hand toward the floor, trying to calm his Reapers down. He once again addresses Naomi, "Will that be all, madam?"

"Yes," Naomi says. "You are free to go. An official copy of President Mason's pardon needs all of your signatures before you leave town. I expect everyone back here tomorrow morning at ten o'clock. Agreed?"

"Yes, madam. We'll be here at ten sharp. Thank you again."

Wolverine nods, turns to face his Reapers, and waves a hand toward the door. Professor snaps back from this stunned outburst and begins walking toward the council room main doors mumbling angrily about the council's decision and even Wolverine's acceptance.

As the Reapers stroll down the long corridor to the front doors, Wolverine's mind reflects on just how lucky they are. *I'm sad to lose Doc and Professor for a year, but excited that they will have an opportunity to make remarkable improvements on the security at Area 51. I bet they'll even get to work on some very advanced aircraft, something they'll both love.*

"Hell, after a year, I might not be able to entice them back," he mumbles to himself with a chuckle.

Wolverine is grateful for the opportunity to continue their mission as a global anti-terrorist organization. It will take time to get used to the new chain-of-command, but he actually relishes the idea of bringing the GDO to a more noticeable or potentially even more prominent position in the global community.

Looks as if I'm moving, he thinks with a grin ... *to the Netherlands. I hope PVL doesn't mind my company until I get a place of my own,* he finishes.

The Reapers all exit into the NATO+ front circular lot. The crisp, clean evening Belgium air rushes to fill their lungs. All four seem to simultaneously inhale a deep breath, hold it for just a second, and then exhale ... almost in unison.

Looking up at the stars, Wolverine's thoughts drift to Jorge Valdez and Esteban Bertiz. At the same time, he realizes that as soon as the world eradicates one roach, another is right there to take its place.

He slowly nods, almost instinctually, as a sign of acceptance. For his destiny, his commitment is to give the world hope that one day everyone will live in peace … free from the roaches that threaten the world.

Robert Grand

Author, Publisher & Aerospace Engineer

Robert's inspiration for the Reaper Two-Six series of novels came from his first love — flying. From a young age, airplanes secured a special place in his heart. After high school, Robert attended The University of Texas at Austin and graduated with a Bachelor's Degree in Aerospace Engineering in 1988. Even though working on exciting F-15 projects at McDonnell Douglas was very rewarding, his heart ached for the thrill and passion of piloting an aircraft. Finally, his dream came true when he earned a private pilots' license, giving him the pure enjoyment of commanding a Grumman Tiger Aircraft.

During his 25 years in engineering, Robert worked for a number of aeronautical companies: McDonnell Douglas, Cirrus Design, NASA, Eaton, and Pratt & Whitney. Supporting programs like the advanced F-15 design and testing, Space Shuttle flight path evaluation, ST-50 proof-of-concept design and testing, and jet engine overhaul and repair, Robert loved seeing the fruits of his labor take to the skies. As life in southeast Michigan changed, Robert took upon new career challenges; applying his diverse engineering background in the automotive industry. He spent the past 13 years involved with the design, development and testing of steering systems.

Contact Robert at productions@reapertwosix.com or visit his website at www.reapertwosixproductions.com.

Made in the USA
Charleston, SC
09 October 2013